"We need a man!"

"Oh, dear, Kitty, I do believe it's too late for you to start worrying about that," Swinnie said. "You're a bit past your childbearing years, hon."

"I know that!" Kitty didn't appreciate that remark, and injected her tone with plenty of disdain. "I meant *for Mary*."

"Mary!" Tom repeated with astonishment.

"Mary!" Bert echoed.

"Mary?" Swinnie asked. "What would she do with a man?"

"Why, make a family, of course!" Outraged, Kitty stared across the barrel where the dominoes lay, still mostly unplayed. How could her friends not see the brilliance of her suggestion? "Finding her a man might keep her here."

The door swung open suddenly, sending dust flying from the shade and startling the four downcast occupants of the store. The tallest, most gorgeous man Kitty had ever laid eyes on walked inside.

"Turn on the air-conditioning so we can get some circulation in here, Bert," she instructed with a gleam in her eye. "Sir, you've come to the right place!"

ABOUT THE AUTHOR

Tina Leonard loves to laugh, which is one of the many reasons she loves writing Harlequin American Romance books! In another lifetime Tina thought she would be single and an East Coast fashion buyer forever. The unexpected happened when Tina met Tim again after many years—she hadn't seen him since they'd attended school together from first through eighth grade. They married, and now Tina keeps a close eye on her school-age children's friends! Lisa and Dean keep their mother busy with soccer, gymnastics and horseback riding. They are proud of their mom's "kissy books" and eagerly help her any way they can. Tina hopes that readers will enjoy the love of family she writes about in her books. Recently, a reviewer wrote, "Leonard has a wonderful sense of the ridiculous," which Tina loved so much she wants it for her epitaph. Right now, however, she's focusing on her wonderful life and writing a lot more romance!

Books by Tina Leonard

HARLEQUIN AMERICAN ROMANCE

A Match
Made in Texas

TINA LEONARD

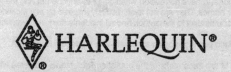

HARLEQUIN®

TORONTO • NEW YORK • LONDON
AMSTERDAM • PARIS • SYDNEY • HAMBURG
STOCKHOLM • ATHENS • TOKYO • MILAN • MADRID
PRAGUE • WARSAW • BUDAPEST • AUCKLAND

ISBN 0-373-16796-2

A MATCH MADE IN TEXAS

Copyright © 1999 by Tina Leonard.

This edition published by arrangement with Harlequin Books S.A.

® and TM are trademarks of the publisher. Trademarks indicated with ® are registered in the United States Patent and Trademark Office, the Canadian Trade Marks Office and in other countries.

Visit us at www.romance.net

Printed in U.S.A.

To Lisa and Dean, I love you; thank you both for helping Mom on the Happy Leonard Family Road Tour. Many thanks to my husband, Tim, who believes in me and doesn't mind driving. Mimi and Dad, my kids will always have good memories of that trip because you were there—your support means so much.

Many, many thanks to my sister, Kim Eickholz, who constantly answered my questions about medical education, etc. I love you.

And to my editor, Denise O'Sullivan, who has faith in me and guides me to achieve.

Chapter One

Mary, Mary, Quite Contrary,
How does your garden grow?

The mayor of Sunflower Junction and owner of Bert's Bait Shop & Gas Station sighed as he looked out the window of his tiny, somewhat odoriferous store. "The van Doorn sisters have been to church again," Bert Fielder observed.

His best friends, Kitty, Tom and Swinnie, barely looked up from their dominoes. The van Doorn girls had been spending a lot of time at the church and cemetery since their folks had passed away at the beginning of the summer. It was a darn shame, but Kitty thought the girls were bearing up well. Particularly the eldest, Mary. She had quite a burden to shoulder with all those siblings to look after now. Kitty sighed. Mary was twenty-seven. Her sisters Rachel, Joan, Eve, Juliet, Antoinette and Esther, respective ages twenty-five, twenty-three, twenty-one, a double nineteen for the twins Juliet and Antoinette, and then the baby, Esther, seventeen, would try the sanity of saints. They were all good girls and Kitty loved each of them, but lately she didn't sleep well wondering how they'd get along without their parents' firm, caring hands guiding them.

The van Doorns had been scrupulous planners in everything, including spacing their children two years apart—except for the year they'd had twins, which a person might expect to throw them off course for a bit.

But no. The van Doorns had loved their daughters mightily. They had been intent on a large, boisterous family.

It was going to be a lot for studious Mary to handle. Still, the young woman possessed common sense and intelligence. Surely it would all work out for them.

"Reckon they'll sell the farm now," Bert said dolefully.

Kitty May was the only realtor in Sunflower Junction. In a town that boasted one stoplight, there wasn't much call for buying and selling property. "Mary hasn't spoken to me about an appraisal for her farm. Maybe they won't sell. Maybe they'll stay here," she said hopefully.

"I hope they do," Swinnie Hopkins agreed. She thumped a domino on the table and adjusted her silver-rimmed bifocals. "Won't be the same without them."

Tom Shoemaker leaned back in the wooden slat-backed chair, his mind thoroughly off dominoes and onto the sisters. "Don't think they will stay," he commented. "Mary needs to finish her residency. She'll have to go back to California for that." He eyed his coffee mug as if there might be answers in the dark liquid. "Much as I hate to say it, we haven't got much here for those youngsters."

Silence fell upon the smelly, dusty bait shop. Outside, the sound of the van Doorn sisters calling to each other as they spied in the windows of long-closed shops along the town square added to the melancholy mood in the room.

"I remember when they was all just knee-high to pups," Bert murmured.

"Yep. We don't even need a public school now that they're all grown," Tom observed. "The van Doorns *were* the town of Sunflower Junction."

It was a sad but true fact. After the oil bust of the eighties, people who had come to the small town to look for oil had left dry. All that beautiful black oil was sixty miles to the east, and not a drop to be had in the vicinity. Just like after the heyday of the California gold rush, shops in the town had closed, and the happy noise of children had long since left the schoolyard.

"Darn it," Swinnie muttered. "It's going to be bad when they go."

Who knew what would happen to the lovely sunflowers that stood tall and brightly cheerful against the hot July sun once the sisters vacated the farm? For years, the main commerce in Sunflower Junction had been the van Doorn sunflower fields, and a wondrous bounty it had provided.

"Not to mention the sisters *are* the tax rolls," Kitty observed. "And the greater portion of the 'twenty' on the population sign."

The pretty sign painted with sunflowers, which welcomed visitors to the town, proclaimed a population of twenty-two—but that was before the van Doorn parents' demise. Bert hadn't been able to bring himself to order a new sign yet. "I remember when we had a bank here, and a restaurant other than the Shotgun Diner." He cracked his knuckles. As mayor, he felt it incumbent upon himself to look after the well-being of the dried-up town. But he was at a loss as to how to deal with the dilemma they faced.

The door opened suddenly with a wheezy creak, and the van Doorn sisters spilled in.

"Hi, everybody!" Mary called. Her sisters filed behind her, wearing freshly pressed church dresses and looking like a garden of summer flowers. "What are you all up to?"

Bert, Swinnie, Kitty and Tom glanced at each other with some uneasy trepidation.

"Dominoes," Kitty said swiftly, thinking that was partially the truth.

"Hmm." Mary eyed the table where only about eight of the black pieces lay played. "Game not going too well?"

"We got sidetracked," Bert offered. "Where are y'all off to?"

"Home," Mary answered.

The four townspeople shared worried glances. How long would that be the van Doorn homestead, anyway? They didn't dare ask. At summer's end, Mary surely would return to California, and Rachel, Joan and Eve would return to the colleges they attended.

"We're thinking about frying up some chicken." Mary ran a palm fondly over Bert's thinly haired pate. "Would you four care to join us?"

It just about put tears in Kitty's eyes. The child

was so good, so thoughtful. So sensible. Her parents had instilled that in her, and in all of her siblings. There wasn't a bad blossom in the whole bouquet of sisters. "I'm in the mood for chicken," she answered gratefully. "I'll bring potato salad."

"I'll bring brownies," Swinnie offered. She was proud of her brownies which won ribbons every year at the State Fair of Texas.

"I'll bring my latest gizmo." Tom smiled proudly. "It's a sunbeamer. You put it in your kitchen, and when the sun comes up in the morning it activates the beamer, which in turn starts your coffeemaker and, once I perfect it, possibly other appliances."

Not to be outdone, Bert rushed to speak. "I'll bring, uh—" Bert threw a quick, desperate look around his bait shop "uh—"

"Just yourselves," Mary said with a sweet smile. "That's all we want."

"We've got everything taken care of," Esther, the baby, added.

The sisters began leaving, one after another, taking the sunshine they'd brought into the dim, stale bait store with them.

"Come at six," Mary said, dropping a kiss on each wrinkled cheek.

She exited, and the door closed with a soft slam.

Swinnie wiped sentimental moisture from under her bifocals. "Such good girls."

"Just like their parents," Kitty agreed, her throat tight. "Going to have us four old fogeys over for Sunday supper. Of course, we're all the family they have now."

"True." Bert hitched up his pants and went to

lower the rickety shade on the door. Now that the girls had paid their visit, there likely wouldn't be any more people meandering into his store. He might as well close up and go home to wait for supper.

"They're all the family *we* have," Swinnie said softly.

The thought of losing the sisters hung heavy in the room.

"I suppose we're being selfish." Kitty wanted to cry but she wouldn't allow herself to. It was too darn hot to get all salty. "There's nothing for them here, but I don't want them to leave."

Tom sighed, unable to put voice to his emotions.

Bert scratched his rapidly balding hairline. "Surely there's something we can do."

The fish freezer rattled in the corner, finishing on a moan that signaled its age. A fly buzzed, trapped up under the shade Bert had lowered.

"We need a man!" Kitty announced, snapping her fingers.

"Oh, dear, I do believe it's too late for you to start worrying about that," Swinnie said. "You're a bit past your childbearing years, hon."

"I know that!" Kitty didn't appreciate that remark, and injected her tone with plenty of disdain. "I meant for *Mary.*"

"Mary!" Tom repeated with astonishment.

"Mary!" Bert echoed.

"Mary?" Swinnie asked. "What would she do with a man?"

"Why, make a family, of course!" Outraged, Kitty stared across the barrel where the dominoes lay, still mostly unplayed. How could her friends not see the brilliance of her suggestion?

"Mary's going to be a doctor," Swinnie pointed out reasonably. "She's not getting married."

"That's right," Tom agreed. "She's too smart for any man."

"Sunflower Junction could use a doctor just as much as San Diego or any other big city," Kitty said defensively. "Finding her a man might keep her here."

Her idea didn't meet with enthusiasm. Nobody wanted to put word to the truth of what they were all thinking. To do so would be to speak ill of a girl they all loved. But the long and the short of it was that Mary van Doorn was perhaps...homely. Middle-of-the-range attractive, scoring squarely around a five on a scale of ten. It wasn't fair. All the other siblings were blessed with their share of eye-pleasing qualities. But Mary was tall, with a figure that could only be called wonderfully ripe. Not stocky, mind you, but filled out with the healthy attributes of her Dutch ancestors. Her hair, while long to her waist and kissed by golden sunshine, was straight as an ironing board. Her lovely aquamarine eyes, which forever sparkled with intelligence and kindness, were hidden behind studious-looking tortoiseshell glasses. Tiny freckles played across her nose and cheeks, highlighting wonderful cheekbones, but what man cared about bones? On the good side of the ledger, she'd never need a nose job for her delicate nose, nor collagen injections, because her lips were full and melted into generous smiles.

But Mary van Doorn's best attribute was her sweet

and caring personality, and men these days didn't seem to care much beyond the bait. Though Mary didn't worry about setting her bait out right. She didn't dress fashionably, she wore little if any makeup and no jewelry.

No, she would never stop traffic in a one-stoplight town.

Kitty sighed, almost defeated. "I guess what made me think of trying to find her a husband was that I had a man call me today at the office."

"A man!" Swinnie sat up straight. "Whatever for?"

"He was inquiring as to the availability of property in Sunflower Junction." Kitty's tone conveyed her surprise at receiving the phone call.

"Really?" Tom and Bert were agog at this news.

"Does he fish?" Bert wanted to know.

"I didn't ask that!" Kitty retorted.

"How old is he?" Swinnie inquired.

"I didn't ask that, either!" Kitty was about thoroughly put out. "The first person who's called my office in a quarter of a year might have gotten scared off by me asking for his private details!"

"Well, you might have asked if he fishes," Bert said on a sigh.

"It doesn't matter." Kitty got to her feet. "He's not coming here. We don't have anything that might interest him."

"Oh." The three faces at the table fell like a cake gone flat in the oven.

"I was thinking about properties, not Mary," she said thoughtfully. "Although Mary wouldn't be interested in a man, and I doubt very seriously she'd catch the eye of some city businessman who's looking for a weekend retreat. Even if he was available, and eligible, and those are big ifs.'' Defeated, she reached for the door handle. All she could do was go home and make potato salad, which didn't seem like the kind of help Mary needed.

"Well, there're other men," Bert said hopefully. "Lots of fish in the sea, y'know."

His bait shop/gas station was located just off the highway. Someone might come through one day for gas who would be right for Mary, though Bert estimated he got about one customer a month. That was twelve chances a year, he calculated rapidly.

Trouble was, Mary would leave at the end of the summer. One month.

"I know miracles happen all the time," Kitty murmured. "We could have one yet." Of course, what she'd liked most about her unexpected caller was his name. *Jake Maddox,* he'd said, in a deliciously warm tone guaranteed to make a woman sigh with expectation. His voice projected authority, yet managed to make her think that he must be a very handsome, very delectable man.

It wasn't until now that she'd realized she liked his voice so much that she hadn't stopped thinking about it. Then Mary had walked in with her sisters, and the answer had been obvious.

Mary needed a man with strength and compassion, who would love her for the special woman she was.

The door swung open suddenly, sending dust flying from the shade and startling the four downcast occupants of the store. The tallest, most gorgeous man Kitty had ever laid eyes on walked inside.

"Can you folks tell me if the real-estate agency next door is closed?" the big-shouldered, confident male asked.

Kitty's mouth dropped open. She needed no name to know that this man was Jake Maddox! That voice was too wonderful to be forgotten. Miracles did happen, even in Sunflower Junction!

"Turn on the air conditioning so we can get some circulation in here, Bert," she instructed with a gleam in her eye. "Sir, believe it or not, you've come to the right place!"

IF MARY VAN DOORN had learned one thing in her twenty-seven years, it was that organization was key. There could be no deviation from the outline, the schedule. Life could turn into a disaster if one didn't adhere to the set timetable. Her parents had raised her with an appreciation for doing things just so; they had reared a family and built a successful business on this ideology. With a formulated plan set out for her, Mary approached college and med school with a practiced ease her peers envied. She stuck to her plan, and left little margin for error.

Mary had six siblings to oversee now. She wasn't about to deviate from that which had stood her in good stead all of her life. Their little family had this one last summer to enjoy the farm where they'd grown up—and then, unfortunately, Sunflower Acres would have to be sold. With four of the sisters attending college, and the twins ready to do likewise, only Esther was left with a year of high school remaining. Mary intended to see that all of her sisters were launched into appropriate curricula, and once each had left the proverbial nest and was on her way to a successful career, she would feel satisfied that she had done her duty.

It was devastating to leave behind a home they all loved, but the fact was that Sunflower Acres couldn't be run unless they were all here to help with the tending and selling of the family product. Mary had a year of residency in California before she could finally begin a practice, so that left her unavailable to oversee the farm. Though they had plenty of money from the farm's prosperity, that money should be spent on the girls' education. Their parents had wanted all of them to receive excellent schooling.

Mary did not intend to forsake her parents' formula. It had secured her goals to this point and would work as well for her sisters.

There would be, perhaps, a tiny uproar when her siblings learned of her plans to sell the farm, but in the end, no doubt they would see the practicality of her plan.

As she pulled an apple pie from the oven, Mary told herself the blast of heat from inside was what started her tears. Setting the pie on two trivets to cool, she grabbed a tissue and furiously wiped at her eyes. But her nose began running, so she had to reach for another tissue, and before she knew it, she was crying so hard she decided she might as well give in to it all the way.

This sentimental attack was not in her plans for the evening. But she couldn't stop. Allowing herself to fall into the nearest kitchen chair, Mary cried out all the fear and loneliness she felt at being responsible for her sisters. She wept all the tears over her parents' deaths she hadn't had time to weep because she was comforting her sisters and making funeral arrangements. In their time of grief, Mary had been strong for her family. Her parents would have wanted that. She would not have wanted them to be anything other than proud.

Laying her head on the table next to the cheery napkin-wrapped basket of chicken she'd fried only a half hour ago and set out for her guests, Mary wondered if she could accomplish all the dreams her parents had wanted for the girls.

"Yoo-hoo! Mary! Yoo-hoo!"

The front hallway filled with the sounds of suddenly arriving guests. Mary shot to her feet, realizing at once she couldn't get to a mirror before they saw her tear-swollen face. "Rats!" she muttered, snapping on the cold-water tap. She splashed cold water over her face, hoping to cool the redness which was surely there. Her nose felt like a balloon! Snatching a paper towel, she dried off her face, smoothed a hand over her hair, and went out to greet them as a proper hostess should. At least it was only the four people who had known her since she was in diapers. They wouldn't mind her blotchy face, Mary comforted herself.

They stood in the hallway, smiling at her with fond expressions. "Mary," Kitty announced with delight, "we've brought a guest to dinner!"

She stepped aside, and seemed to pull a man from nowhere. Mary's lips parted.

He was simply the most handsome man she had ever laid eyes on. Her heart began a nervous beat inside her as she took in how tall he was, much taller than Bert and Tom, who stood off to the side grinning like they were keeping a secret. Swinnie's eyes were huge, as if she'd just won the prize at the fair again for the brownies she clutched on a white plate in front of her. Kitty just grinned hugely.

The stranger smiled at Mary, a slow, dawning smile of pleasure that spoke of good manners, and extended his hand.

"I'm Jake Maddox," he said in a wonderfully deep, soothing voice that sent unexpected chills running up the backs of her bare legs.

Still in shock, Mary took his hand, registering only that it was warm and firm as he nodded at her with a sexy grin. Richly dark hair in a nice cut made her think he probably looked as good in a business suit as in the khaki pants he was currently wearing. Deepest blue eyes and a strong chin reminded her of a boy she'd had a crush on in grade school—only there was nothing boyish about this big man. He was at least her father's height and maybe better, which meant that she had to look up into those indigo-blue eyes. She couldn't remember the last time she'd met a man who was so solidly built that he made her feel like a doll, she of the dratted long limbs and over-ripe curves.

Suddenly, she remembered to let go of his hand. The dizzying rush of her blood didn't stop. Remembering that her nose was swollen and her cheeks damp, Mary took the plate of brownies from Swinnie's hands and headed to the kitchen to catch her breath.

A dinner guest named Jake Maddox was definitely *not* in the plans.

JAKE MADDOX watched as his attractive hostess disappeared into a room off the hallway, her nicely tanned and healthy legs hurrying so that the just-under-knee-length skirt of her blue-and-white sundress swished. Bert looked up at him expectantly.

"I told you Mary would consider it her community obligation and a pleasure to welcome someone who was considering making Sunflower Junction his home," Bert said with an expansive grin.

Jake wasn't so sure that was what the woman's reaction had been. Certainly, she had given every impression that she *meant* to be welcoming, but she'd seemed rather startled as well. Kitty and Swinnie glanced at each other, excused themselves and headed into the same area of the house his hostess had gone. Tom nodded reassuringly at him.

"Yes, she's plenty glad to have you." He verified Bert's statement without blinking.

They disappeared into a large, flower-decorated den. Jake felt his only option was to follow them, though he would have preferred to have gone where the women were so he could help out with whatever needed to be done. As much as the sign at the end of the drive had proclaimed "Welcome to Sunflower Acres," Jake felt like an interloper.

But Tom and Bert appeared to be right at home. They switched on the television with a remote, and gestured at Jake to sit down.

"Take a load off," Mayor Bert instructed him. "Mary'll give a good shout when it's time to put on the feed bag."

"Yep," Tom verified.

Jake shifted his eyes in impatience, though it was

clear he had been relegated to male-bonding since the females hadn't issued him an invitation to join them. Fighting off the feeling that he should be doing something in exchange for his obviously unexpected appearance, Jake sat.

He wasn't interested in watching "The Price Is Right," which had Tom and Bert guessing dollar amounts with great relish. Glancing around the den, he decided the van Doorn family had been very close. Pictures of a lot of babies and girls in several growing stages adorned the walls. A collection of pewter frames held more photos. Over the fireplace, an enormous professional portrait showed the family to be a large and happy one. Seven girls, and a proud mother and father.

It was a lot of children, Jake decided. But the parents looked happy about their situation. A lot happier than he was at the prospect that he was going to be raising one.

One boy. His sister, Steffie, had decided that babies grew into toddlers with tantrums and she couldn't deal with it anymore. Steffie had called him in tears, told him she wanted more out of life than she'd gotten so far with an unplanned teenage pregnancy, and was putting the boy up for adoption. Steffie had whimsically named her baby Cruise Gibson Maddox after two movie stars she thought were handsome.

Jake grimaced. Finally realizing that his sister was serious about the adoption plan and that their mother had no intention of helping her since "she got herself into that boat; she'll have to row it," Jake decided to take matters into his own hands.

Cruise was three now, and according to Steffie, a

handful she couldn't wait to relinquish. This handful he was about to receive was the reason for his visit to Sunflower Junction. Since his nephew had not known stability, Jake was determined to give him that now. A house in the country, where they could get away from the rush of the city, and the frenzied approach to life. Jake and Cruise were going to get to know each other and be close—the way Steffie, Jake and their parents had never been.

What the van Doorns obviously had managed in their home was pretty much what he'd like for himself and Cruise. Stability and warmth. Love. Respect. Calm.

"Yoo-hoo!" Kitty called. "Time to eat!"

Jake got to his feet, looking forward to seeing his hostess again. Following Kitty into the kitchen without waiting for Bert and Tom to hop up from their appointed chairs, Jake held his breath in anticipation.

The kitchen was full of women, all talking and moving things from counter to table with a swiftness that paralyzed him.

"Everybody, this is Jake!" Mary called over the din.

A murmured chorus of hellos rose to his ears, but that slight pause was the only break in the motion. There apparently was a procedure to be followed. He watched in amazement as several women and the four companions who'd brought him snatched plates, silverware and pre-poured glasses of tea from a kitchen counter. Moving in a line, they served themselves from identical plastic bowls on the next counter, then seated themselves in places where they apparently always sat. There was absolutely no break in the rhythm, so Jake grabbed a plate and juggled his way through the food line, cracking his ankle painfully against a chair leg as he slid into an available place just as every head bowed for grace.

At this moment, he was just grateful that he'd made it in time for the beginning. Bert did a proud oration of grace in the suddenly hushed room, and then the uproar began again. To his dismay, Jake realized he hadn't appropriated a pre-poured tea glass. He glanced at his hostess, who was seated next to him. He wondered if he dared upset the routine by getting up and getting one.

Mary's eyes met his. They softened for just an instant behind her glasses as she noticed his unease. She had gorgeous eyes. He was aware of the urge to reach over and stroke one hand through her hair and slip her glasses off with the other just so he could kiss her and find out if those lips were really as soft as they looked.

"Jake, is there something I can get you?" she asked.

"I forgot my tea, but I can get it myself, thanks." He forced a smile onto his face and stretched his arm over a sister's shoulder to grab a glass from the counter.

For the first time, Mary smiled at him. "Excuse me, everyone," she said loudly. "I just realized we're treating Jake like part of the family."

The diners paused and stared at him as if they were seeing him for the first time.

"I think we should take a break from routine and let everyone introduce themselves." Mary pointed at a sister. "You start, Rachel."

Rachel lowered her fork to her plate. "I'm Rachel, as you just heard Mary say," she said, obviously wondering why she had to repeat that. "It's nice to meet you." She gave the sister next to her an elbowing as she smiled beautifully at Jake.

"I'm Joan," that sister said on a wince and then a well-mannered smile.

"I'm Eve," the next one said.

"We're Juliet and Antoinette," a pair of girls spoke in unison, obviously used to doing this.

"And I'm Esther, the last name you have to try to remember," the sister seated to his left said with a bright smile. "You'll hear Miss Kitty refer to me as Esther, the baby, quite often." She laughed and reached to gently squeeze Miss Kitty's shoulder as if she didn't mind the tag.

"I'm Jake Maddox," he said to the room at large. "I appreciate you all having me over for dinner."

They waited, seeming to take their cue from Mary who hadn't begun to eat again. He felt like a new species of bug under a microscope.

But Mary smiled at him with a goodness that went straight to his heart. "Forgive our regimentation. We're so accustomed to it we don't realize we're overwhelming."

He nodded. "It's fine. I'd already decided I'd better not get under anyone's feet."

Mary laughed, and picked up her fork. Obviously relieved, the other sisters did as well and the noise level increased substantially again, making him feel a bit less uncomfortable. It was much better not to be an audience of one to the curious van Doorn clan. He hadn't been examined so closely in boardroom meetings!

Still, there was a method to the madness, he noted as dinner progressed. The group worked together well. There was respect and love in abundance. They clearly didn't think anything odd about including five extra people in their clan as long as the expected routine wasn't interrupted.

Mary's gaze met his, holding a second past a casual glance. With a start, Mary reached for her fork, sending his tea glass spilling across the tabletop. Tea spread into the lace cloth, like an ominous feeling wrecking a perfectly good day. He watched pink embarrassment delicately color her cheeks—and realized he had thrown a kink into Mary's evening.

"I'll get you another."

She tossed a dish towel over the tea stain and jumped to get him another glass before he could move. Quite obviously, his presence at her dinner table made her nervous for some reason.

Meeting her was certainly the last thing he'd expected today when he'd decided to drive out to Sunflower Junction.

He warned himself not to be so intrigued. He was in deep enough with a troubled nephew coming into his life. No sense digging himself in *all* the way over his head.

But throwing Mary off balance would be a challenge and a lot of fun. He couldn't remember ever meeting a woman with a real blush.

He found that very, *very* intriguing.

Chapter Two

"The problem with Mary," Kitty stated the following day as the four friends sat in Bert's Bait Shop & Gas Station, "is that, sweet as she is, she's contrary. Plain, mule-headed contrary!"

Taking that handsome specimen of a man, Jake Maddox, over to meet Mary was an exercise Kitty need not have gotten her girdle out of shape over. Mary had barely paid attention to him—and then there was the disastrous moment at dinner when she'd knocked over his tea. Poor girl had just lost all co-ordination! "Bless her if she didn't look like she'd been rubbing pink watermelon juice across her eyes when we got there," she complained. "How's she going to get a man if she doesn't take better care of her skin?"

Bert looked up from where he was dusting off the tops of soup cans. "Mary's not looking for a man. We're looking for one for her," he reminded the room at large. "We can hardly criticize that she's not gussied up when we sabotage her."

Swinnie puffed out her cheeks, sharing annoyance with Kitty. "Still, she hardly looked at him! You'd think a hunk like that would have even a bookworm like her swooning!''

Kitty sucked her teeth with disgust. "Picky and contrary, that's what Mary van Doorn is! Picky is worse than contrary! Why, in my day, any man with money was a good man.'' She made a wide sweep with her hand.

"Guess our town sign will always read 'Pop. 22,''' Tom intoned.

"Oh, fiddle," Bert complained, knowing very well he should be ordering a sign that said "Pop. 20.'' That was an unhappy thought he could barely face. "Are y'all a bunch of quitters?''

"Quitters!'' Kitty rounded on him. "Did I see you on your rear end watching 'The Price Is Right' while you could have been showing Mr. Maddox those wonderful sunflower fields back of the house? That might have encouraged him to speak up a bit more.'' She crossed her arms. "That boy sat in his chair like a great bump on a log, just staring at Mary, until it was time to leave.''

Bert held up a placating hand, a gesture he was proud of from years of holding town-hall meetings. "All I'm suggesting is that Mr. Maddox doesn't have to be the only bump on our town log.''

Swinnie looked at him suspiciously. "Good ones don't just wander in every day," she reminded him.

"We could hunt one up ourselves.'' He nodded outside at the gas pumps. "From the passing-through-town customers I get in a week's time, I could put out the word.''

"What word?'' Kitty put her hands on her hips impatiently. She knew very well how many potential candidates were likely to turn off the interstate for gas at Bert's. "That we're on a manhunt? That ought to bring the men running like turkeys to a turkey shoot!"

"Well, what about...what about..." Bert fumbled, his grand idea running out of steam.

"Putting up a sign on the highway?" Tom suggested. "Great small town is looking for buyers for great real estate? Then we could drag Mary over to meet any good ones we get."

"No." Kitty shook her head. "We tried that in '95 when we were looking to unload the Widow Stanton's property for her kin. Didn't get taker number one."

It was true. Finally, they'd had to sell the property at auction. The farmer next door had bought it to grow more cotton on, and let the house fall to rack and ruin. At the price he'd paid, it was cheaper to do that.

"Well, I've run out of ideas," she said sourly. "I'm going to work. Let me know if any Prince Charmings stop in to buy gas."

She put plenty of sarcasm in that comment and headed next door to her office.

AN HOUR LATER, Kitty nearly fainted when the real-estate office door suddenly flung open.

An agitated Bert hurried in. "I've found him, I've found him!"

"Who?"

"The perfect man for Mary!" Bert pinwheeled his arms. "Come on!"

She shot to her feet to follow. Outside at the pumps was a motorcycle that had obviously broken down.

The rider looked hot and weary—but with his dark, longish hair and mischievous eyes, Kitty could definitely see his appeal. He seemed a little rougher around the edges than she might have liked, but when he stood as she approached, she thought he at least had good manners. After grilling him for about twenty minutes while Bert very slowly called his brother for a spare part for the motorcycle, Kitty learned that the stranger was getting a medical degree and was on a cross-Texas sabbatical before he settled back down to study again in the fall.

"Oh, my," she murmured to Bert as he brought good news about the availability of the spare part. "I'd better get Mary down here right away!"

Hurrying back into her office, she dialed Mary's number. "Oh, Mary, you'll never believe," she said when Mary answered the phone. "We have the most unfortunate soul down here, just suffering in all this heat. I feel so sorry for him! And you know," she whispered confidentially to appeal to the doctor in Mary, "I do believe he looks a mite peaked. Perhaps even dehydrated. It's this darn heat!"

Two minutes later, she hung up, well satisfied. Mary was on the way with some apple pie and refreshingly cold lemonade—and if all went well, she might just pair up with a motorcycle rider who was also a med student, which would give them something in common. He'd mentioned kin in Dallas he'd been visiting—and Kitty thought that boded well for everyone involved.

This was one easy rider who might be convinced to stay in Sunflower Junction—once he met his dream woman.

"CONTRARY!" Kitty cried to Bert, Swinnie and Tom after the motorcycle rider, whose name was Richard, had ridden off with Rachel on the back of his bike. Rachel had offered to show him around Sunflower Junction—and other than offering him the refreshments, Mary hadn't seemed all that interested. "Mary is just as contrary as the day is long! Why, I don't believe she said more than how do you do to that boy!"

"It was obviously a perfectly good plan," Swinnie commiserated with Bert, who looked heartbroken. "Who would ever have dreamed she'd bring her sister with her, and those two would strike up a conversation?"

"Well it was easy for Rachel to do so with Mary standing there like she had lips made of new leather," Kitty complained crossly. "For heaven's sake! How does she expect to ever catch a man if she doesn't talk to one? Doesn't she understand how important it is to flirt? Rachel certainly used the goo-goo eyes on him."

"Mary's not looking for a man," Tom pointed out reasonably.

"Oh, hush!" Kitty didn't want to hear about that. Tom simply didn't understand that at twenty-seven Mary was a bit long in the tooth. With a load of younger sisters, she had built-in competition. Full of a mother's affection for her most-beloved child, Kitty could hardly bear for her eldest goddaughter to have such wallflower tendencies.

Surely the right man would turn up sooner than later.

"WELL, THAT'S A FINE kettle of fish!" Kitty snapped a week later as she hung up the phone. "Rachel rode off to Montana with that easy rider you shanghaied, Bert."

Three heads whipped around to stare at her. The domino game lost every bit of interest it had held a second ago.

"What?" Bert demanded.

Kitty nodded at the shock on all their faces. "You heard me. She eloped with that boy, and she won't be coming back." She gave the group a sad shake of her head. "That's one van Doorn out of the coop."

Bert scratched at his bald spot. That meant the sign he needed to order should read "Pop. 19."

It was too dismal to think about.

"I've got another plan," he said desperately. "This one's sure to work!"

He winced under the scrutiny of sardonically raised eyebrows. "We need to have us a wife raffle."

"A wife raffle!" Kitty snorted. "We've only got one woman we want to make a wife. One prize."

"Just listen!" He waved her comment aside. "We put up a billboard and run some advertisements in Dallas about the wife raffle we're having. That ought to bring some tourists in, and surely an eligible bachelor or two."

"Wouldn't it be a husband raffle?" Swinnie wanted this clarified.

"Heck if I know. What I do know is we better not let Mary get wind of this scheme, or she'll be put out with us." Kitty thought Mary's head was so dizzy these days with everything she had on her plate that she wasn't likely to notice if they put *her* up at auction for a million bucks.

"It ain't gonna work," Tom warned them on a sigh. "I foresee turrible trouble with this harebrained idea."

SUNFLOWER JUNCTION put out its finest effort the night of the Great Wife Raffle. The Junior League—or what they called the Junior League here—sunk its teeth into this excellent fund-raising idea and put out calls all over Dallas to well-heeled bachelors. Kitty was extremely proud of her efforts. The town-hall floor shone like a newly minted dime. Windows sparkled with the brilliance of crystal chandeliers. Swinnie had raided Mary's sunflower fields, and the whole room was alight with gorgeous buttercup-yellow and prairie-orange blooms.

Between the two of them and a few women from the church, they had managed to usher every *single* van Doorn girl to the town hall in pretty dresses, and lots of curls in their fabulously blond, long hair. Claiming there was a birthday party for one of the town's few citizens, they had shamelessly used their last scruple to coax Mary away from the ledgers she had studiously been going over. They had even forced her to turn loose of her tortoiseshell glasses.

"I can't see without them!" Mary protested. But she'd gone along with their wish, after they'd promised to lead her everywhere she needed to go—their goal being the stage where the bachelors could get a good eyeful of her.

Mary was in the ladies' room right now, putting on some light lipstick.

"When Mary sees the splendid surprise we have in store for her, she won't be mad at us a bit," Kitty grandly postulated.

"No girl could be, who'd secured a husband for herself," Swinnie agreed.

Several of their friends in Dallas had even come in for the auction. *It's such a success,* Kitty thought with delight, *we ought to do this every year.* Fund-raising was a gift she had in abundance. Every cent of the money earned from tickets and concessions was going for a new roof for the Sunflower Junction courthouse and to a children's charity in Dallas.

It was a night guaranteed to make dreams come true. And when Kitty and Swinnie saw the delicious men in devastatingly dapper business suits arriving, they hugged each other with glee.

"A MORE HEADSTRONG GIRL never lived!" Kitty exclaimed the next day. "Why, Mary van Doorn just plain doesn't *want* to get married!"

They were so downcast, they didn't bother to put out the dominoes. The evening had been a disaster. Oh, plenty of money had been rung up for charity and everyone had enjoyed themselves immensely—but luck of luck, Mary would have nothing to do with getting up on the stage with the Dallas women to be "raffled." Eve had jumped up there with alacrity and been won by a wealthy investment banker.

He had proposed on the spot.

Kitty had nearly stamped her foot with ire. If only Mary had gotten up there!

"Who would have thought Mary would be so obstinate?" Swinnie inquired of nobody in particular.

The bait shop phone rang, startling everyone. Bert went to answer, his expression getting unhappier as the conversation progressed. He hung up and slowly approached the barrel.

"That was Mary."

They all sat up expectantly. "She's still speaking to us, then?" Kitty asked.

"Yes." He sighed and took his seat. "She wanted to let us know that the wedding date for Eve and her investment banker is in a month. Apparently, he wants to take her to Spain for a honeymoon, and this is the best season."

"Oh, Spain," Kitty moaned. "Mary could have had a wonderful time in Spain!"

"Then they're coming home."

"Oh, good!" Swinnie brightened. "So we achieve our goal after all! I don't know about you, but the way that banker fellow was eating Eve up with his eyes, I'd say they'll start populating soon."

"They're coming home means to America." Bert glared at Swinnie. "They intend to move into his mansion in Dallas."

"Dallas!" everyone echoed.

"Yes, and worse, they've invited the twins to stay with them."

"The twins!" Kitty's brows beetled. "Why would a newly married couple want the twins around?"

"Because the banker travels a lot, and the twins saw a picture of his kin. They figure hanging out around a pool in Dallas and at the country club he belongs to is more to their liking than harvesting sunflowers." Bert shook his head.

"Well, that leaves us with Joan, Mary and Esther, the baby." Kitty looked as if she was about to cry.

"Nope." He shook his head. "Joan's leaving for college this week. She's got to take some summer mini-courses."

"Oh." Kitty calculated rapidly. "Oh, no! That leaves us with only two! And Mary won't marry and Esther—well, she's just a *baby*." She looked around at her friends. "We do have *some* integrity."

But that left them with a sign that was going to read "Pop. 15." Mary was independent-minded and financially set, and it appeared that no amount of chicanery was going to get her into a white gown and veil.

"I warned y'all," Tom reminded them. "All your meddling's lost us five of the van Doorns. You're just lucky Mary and Esther are still around."

"I surely thought that Jake Maddox was the right one," Kitty murmured. "Never saw a man eyeball a woman like he did Mary."

The phone rang again. Bert got up to answer. After a moment, he hung up. Kitty could see the tears sparkling in his eyes.

"That was Mary again. She says she'd like you to come over and hang a "For Sale" sign in the yard, Kitty. With all the girls gone, she'll not be able to do the harvest by herself, and as she says, the house is too big for just her and Esther." Misery was deep in his face. "Guess that'll bring the sign down to 'Pop. 13' in no time."

Kitty could almost hear her own heart shattering to pieces. She didn't think she could bear it if Mary and Esther left Sunflower Junction. The others were great girls and she loved them like daughters—but Mary and Esther, well, those girls had been the lights in her eyes for as long as she could remember.

And now they were going to leave her.

Chapter Three

Jake waited apprehensively at the airport for his nephew to arrive. Steffie was bringing the child to him, then turning back around on the same plane to return home. He couldn't believe she wouldn't even bother to stay over a night to make sure Cruise didn't suffer relocation distress. But that was his family. Distant. Lukewarm at best.

He couldn't help thinking about Mary. He'd thought about her a million times since he'd met her last week. Many times he had nearly called her. With Cruise coming, though, he felt he shouldn't call. It didn't seem fair to involve her in his problem when she obviously had enough on her hands as it was.

But in all his thirty years, Jake couldn't remember ever meeting a woman who'd struck his fancy the way she did. Mary was a gentle soul, and he was looking for that kind of warmth in his life.

The gate suddenly filled with people. A flight attendant deplaned first, holding a little boy by the hand. In her other hand she held up a sign that read, "Maddox."

Astonished, Jake strode forward. "Is this Cruise

Gibson Maddox?" He hadn't seen anything since the baby picture Steffie had sent—the child had grown a lot since then.

"Yes," the flight attendant answered. "Are you here for him?"

"Yes." He glanced around with irritation. "Is his mother still on the plane?" He couldn't believe she wouldn't at least get off to say hello.

"Cruise traveled alone." The flight attendant ruffled the child's hair and bent down to give him a comforting smile. "And you were a big boy, too, weren't you, Cruise?"

"Alone?" Jake roared. "He traveled alone? And you let him?"

The woman froze him with cool gray eyes. "You might talk to the person who paid for the ticket about his traveling circumstances. Now, if I may see your driver's license?"

He whipped it out with irritation. She eyed it—and him—thoroughly. "Thank you," she bit out. "Good-bye, Cruise," she said with a sweet smile for the boy. "Take good care of him," the woman had the nerve to instruct, as if Jake would do anything else. Then she stalked off.

Of course, from her point of view, Cruise didn't appear to be that well cared for, Jake knew. He'd traveled alone on a fifty-minute flight without even a toy as far as he could tell. No doubt the little guy had been scared to death. When Jake talked to his mother and sister next, he was going to let them have it. He stared down at Cruise, and received a baleful look in return.

"Here, Cruise," he said kindly, holding out a

green-and-black hand-sized football he'd brought to smooth the waters. "I'm your Uncle Jake. I'm looking forward to catching some balls with you."

Ignoring the football, Cruise launched a swift kick to Jake's shin. Stars of pain burst behind Jake's eyes.

Suddenly, he wondered how he was going to raise this child.

He had no idea.

MARY COULDN'T REMEMBER a time in her life when she'd felt so lost. She was scared, too. And fiercely worried that she wasn't living up to her parents' wishes as far as the girls were concerned.

So much had happened so quickly that her head was in a whirl. It seemed disastrous that their parents' guidance on the family helm had been snatched away. Mercy! Who would have ever thought Rachel would just jump willy-nilly onto the back of a motorcycle and elope? It made Mary's head hurt. Of course, she'd given Rachel her blessing and kept her misgivings to herself. But a thousand times a day she wondered if their parents would have handled the situation differently.

And now Eve—getting married in a month! Mary rubbed the bridge of her nose where her glasses rested. Planning a wedding was tough work, more nerve-wracking than medical school in some ways. So many details to be worked out! She was trying very hard for Eve's sake to plan a wonderful wedding. The family name was involved, naturally, and Eve wanted everything to be perfect.

Mary sighed. It would only be perfect if their mother were here to organize everything with her meticulous hand. It would only be perfect if their father were here to walk Eve down the aisle. Bert and Tom were sharing the honor, and Mary was grateful, but it wasn't the same.

Tears rose in her eyes that she was glad nobody was around to see. It was Saturday evening, and all her sisters had either gone to a movie, or into Dallas to help Eve shop for her trousseau. Mary had begged off. She needed an evening to think through her responsibilities. Guilt that she had really wanted her sisters to leave so that she could have the house to herself for an evening rose like a cloud to further obscure her thoughts.

She'd just needed time away from all the giddiness, and she wasn't a bad person for needing to be alone without somebody needing something from her every second.

Maybe Miss Kitty was right. The Realtor had refused to list the house and put Sunflower Acres up for sale. She'd insisted that Mary was trying to do too much, too fast, too soon. New grief and new responsibilities were enough to handle. She shouldn't sell the last emotional touchstone the sisters shared.

Still, Mary didn't see how she could keep from putting the farm on the market. The business demanded every ounce of energy from everyone during the harvest season, and only she and Esther likely would be here then. Past that, the house would be empty, unless Mary gave up her year of residency...which might actually be more fair to Esther because then she could finish her senior year of high school with her friends. Senior year was so important.

Life had never been so out of control, so frantically awry.

Her thoughts strayed to Jake Maddox. That thought had her jumping out of her skin even more. Something about him had unsettled her in an anticipatory sort of way, as if she'd held her breath and never breathed from the moment he walked in until he'd left after dinner.

How could I have knocked over his tea glass?

The memory brought a burn of mortification to her cheeks. She was never polished, never sophisticated, but for some reason, that night she'd been butterfingers plain and simple. She'd felt so self-conscious! His gaze had been on her constantly, he'd tried to draw her into conversation plenty of times, and her tongue tied itself up in a tight ribbon. Her elbow bumped his forearm a couple of times. She was gawky and long-limbed, she knew, but just for once she wished her elbows would have stayed where they belonged.

Mary took off her glasses and rubbed her eyes. He had not called her. "It was a foolish fantasy you had that he would, Mary van Doorn," she berated herself. Handsome men like Jake did not phone studious types like her. They pursued women who fit into sports cars like tiny dolls, women who knew how to "make conversation."

The phone on the desk rang, startling her clean out of her wits. Probably because her mind had been on Jake, she snatched it up with anticipation.

"Mary?" Kitty's soprano voice sang in her ear.

Mary held back a groan of disappointment. When

would she ever learn to stop daydreaming? "Hi, Miss Kitty."

There was a pause. "What...is something the matter, Mary?"

She sighed to herself over the well-meaning inquisition. Couldn't a person even feel sorry for herself for one evening without someone wondering why she wasn't Mary Sunshine? "Everything's fine, Kitty."

"Oh. Um, where are the girls? I don't hear any excitement in the background."

"They've all gone out, so the excitement level is down a bit." Mary raised her brows, hoping Kitty didn't intend to rush over to provide some excitement for her. She was well aware that Kitty felt she was lacking in the life department. And as her self-appointed mothering role required, Kitty found it necessary to try to provide the things for Mary that she felt she lacked. "I'm enjoying the quiet."

"Oh, you poor dear," Kitty clucked. "No girl enjoys the quiet on a Saturday night. Why I remember those nights myself. Well, there weren't many Saturday nights I was alone, of course. But when the odd one popped up, well, I'd rather have died than for anyone to know I was socially bereft for the evening!"

For some reason, that made Mary laugh. "Don't worry. I'm not about to die over it. Nobody knows except you and me."

"Well—"

She recognized the fret in Kitty's voice. "I won't allow you to worry on my behalf. As you very well know, I have a lot of paperwork to go through and a lot to plan. So don't get yourself in a stew. You just be here tomorrow for Sunday supper and that's plenty of companionship. All right?''

"Well, okay, Mary. But I still think a girl your age ought to be getting out, not sitting in the house like a china statue.''

Mary smiled. She was no knick-knack! "I'll see you tomorrow, then. Thank you for checking on me. Good night, Miss Kitty,'' she said firmly, hanging up.

It was her secret and no one else's, Mary told herself, if she'd wished Jake Maddox might have been on the other end of the phone instead. She wasn't going to feel sorry for herself. There were people in Sunflower Junction who cared about her, sometimes too much. Even Miss Kitty couldn't pull off the impossible feat of conjuring up a dream man for Mary.

"SHE'S OVER THERE ALONE!" Kitty wailed to Bert, Swinnie and Tom. "All of those wretched sisters left her alone to go have fun, and Mary's shut up in the house like a nun!" The realization worried Kitty so much she'd forgotten the original purpose of her phone call, which was to tell Mary that if they were invited over for Sunday supper, she and Swinnie had baked up one heck of a peach pie. They were mighty proud of it, too, and thinking about entering the recipe at the State Fair this year.

"The sisters have to go out sometime," Swinnie pointed out reasonably. "They have wedding preparations to see to.''

"I know." Kitty gnawed on a pencil. "That's what makes it worse. Rachel has a man. Eve has a wedding to plan for. Don't you think Mary's just eating her heart out?''

"No." Bert shook his head. "She seemed happy for her sisters to me. Mostly, anyway. I will say that she appeared a bit unnerved when Rachel rode off into the sunset."

"Yep," Tom agreed. "Don't believe she cared too much for that. At least Rachel had a helmet on, though."

"I know she's happy for them! But I still think it would be hard not to feel a little envy." Kitty nearly had tears in her eyes. "She puts up a good front, but let me tell you, Mary van Doorn has real feelings just like any other woman does."

There was silence in the living room at Kitty's house where the foursome sat desultorily playing bridge. It wasn't really any fun playing when she had so much on her mind.

Bert reached over to pat her hand. "Don't let it bother you. There's nothing we can do about it."

The three of them waited expectantly. Usually, that was how Kitty's best ideas came to light. Someone threw down the gauntlet that "nothing could be done" about a matter, and Kitty would nearly explode with ideas. She hated to feel helpless, and she hated to be wrong. Those were two qualities one could count on getting her worked up good.

Indeed, they could nearly hear the wheels turning in Kitty's mind.

"I'm calling Jake Maddox," she announced.

"No!" the three shouted in unison.

"That's not a good idea," Bert remonstrated. "Come up with a better one. You've been fixated on that man for Mary since you first laid eyes on him."

Kitty jumped to her feet.

Swinnie clapped a hand over her mouth. No one was going to stop her friend now! "You shouldn't have challenged her, Bert!" Swinnie cried. "You know you only challenge when you want her to react!"

"Never mind to all of you," Kitty said, licking her fingers and thumbing swiftly through scribbled notes in her purse.

"It's Saturday night. He's sure to be out with a woman," Tom warned.

"Fine. She won't bother me." Kitty turned the phone on and dialed. "Hello, Jake!" she said merrily, as if he was a long-lost friend. "I hope I'm not interrupting anything?" She gave her cronies a beatific smile. "Oh, good! Listen, I just talked to Mary, and would you believe, she's interested in putting her property on the market?"

Swinnie, Tom and Bert stared at her outright fib. Kitty had told Mary she wouldn't list her property, that it was too soon for her to think of doing such a thing!

"Well, I know it's big, but I also know it's just what you're looking for. After all, you'll have a family of your own one day," she hinted broadly. "And it would get you out of the big city. Not that there's anything wrong with Dallas, mind you. Some of my best friends are from Dallas, you know."

She paused, listening. "I thought you'd feel that way! Shall I show it to you tomorrow, say around four o'clock? I know that's almost suppertime, but it will give you enough time to look around before Mary gets home. She regularly visits the cemeter—I mean, she regularly takes an aerobic walk before she goes home to put the chicken on. Mary's a very healthy girl.''

Her eyebrows rose. ''Oh? You'll miss seeing her?'' She shook a victory fist in the air. Her friends groaned. ''Well, why don't you call her and tell her you'll be out our way tomorrow? Better yet, why don't you join us for supper? Bring something? Why certainly! How about a bucket of chicken from the Colonel's? That way, Mary won't have to cook. What a smart idea of yours. I wish I'd thought of it myself, except we don't have a Colonel's out here. Oh, good. Ta-ta!'' she cried with delight as she hung up the phone. ''There,'' she said proudly, ''don't ever tell me something can't be done!''

That put Bert out. ''Mary's going to be real unhappy with you.''

''Absolutely not! I've found her a man who can bring home his own bacon, and fry the chicken up in the pan.'' Kitty went to refill the tea glasses. ''Or at least buy it fried.''

''What bacon?'' Tom wanted to know. ''This man could be an ax murderer for all we know.''

''Nope!'' Kitty warbled from the kitchen. ''I did some checking on him.''

''I believe it,'' Bert muttered. ''The woman has a nose for matchmaking.''

''Would you believe that Jake Maddox is the son of Deke Maddox, of Maddox Yachts fame? Whose grandfather made his money in railroads—and I don't mean digging the lines for them, either.''

''That means he's wealthy, wealthy, wealthy!'' Swinnie interjected in awe.

''Yes. No fortune-hunter for our Miss Mary. You

have to watch men very carefully these days," Kitty pontificated sagely. "Once upon a time, it was only women who made careers of fortune-hunting. Oh, you had the odd ne'er-do-well of a man, but mostly, it was women who looked for a catch. Equal rights has surely caused a problem for us women," she said on a sigh. "One has to see a man's portfolio and check his birth certificate before one can trust a male nowadays. One almost has to hire a private investigator to make certain nothing unsavory lurks in a man's past, such as ex-wives who've hogged the finances, et cetera."

Swinnie pinned her with a sharp look. "You... didn't."

Kitty batted her eyes at her friends as she set the tea glasses back on the tray. She sat down, totally at peace with herself. "I merely asked some questions which needed answers. I could have been a private investigator in my own right in my younger days. But these aren't my younger days, and truth is, young people don't have the safety of meeting the son-of-the-son-of that we had. Nowadays, one has to take a person at face value with no references, and that could be a bad thing, to my mind. A good P.I. ranks right up there with an angel sitting on my shoulder encouraging my conscience. Now then, Swinnie, if you'll meet me at Mary's about thirty minutes before Jake is to arrive, we'll get her hair in some curlers and sneak a little makeup on her face. Maybe spritz some perfume on her if she'll let us."

"But you told him a lie. You told him Mary was putting her property on the market!" Swinnie was still caught up in the details of the scheme.

"No, I said she was interested in putting her house up. I didn't say she was," Kitty said with authority. "Don't you worry your little head about that. The only thing we've got to market is Mary, and that's the tough job. She's not going to go easily into the beautician's chair." She tapped her nails on the table. "Think we could talk her into taking off her glasses for the evening?

"No," Bert and Tom said at the same time.

"She'd be double-clumsy then. Don't forget the spilled tea," Tom reminded.

"You're right. We're going to have to get that girl some contact lenses." This irritated Kitty, because Mary was one thing she didn't have a whole lot of control over. Contacts were something which didn't interest Mary. She said they made her eyes itch, and she did far too much studying to have scratchy eyes. "Well, pass out the cards," she snapped. "I'm not a miracle-worker, for heaven's sake!"

She wasn't, no matter how much Mary might need her to be one. She could only get the man out there under the most thin ruse.

But she couldn't make them like each other—and the real thing that bothered her about that was Mary. She was as stubborn about men as she was about contacts—determined that she didn't need either one.

MARY'S PHONE RANG AGAIN, and, thinking it was Kitty, she picked it up with a sigh. She'd rather not be harangued any further, but it was eight o'clock in the evening. Her sisters might be calling from one of the stores for advice. "Hello?"

"May I speak to Mary van Doorn, please?"

"This is she," Mary answered, a nervous tremble speeding through her. The man had a wonderful voice.

He sounded very much like Jake Maddox.

"This is Jake," he said, and Mary thought she must be dreaming.

"Hi, Jake." She closed her eyes. "How are you doing?"

"Fine," he replied. "I…well, I had a good time at dinner the other night."

Mary's face warmed as she thought about the unfortunate tea-glass episode. "I'm glad Mayor Bert and crew brought you over. I hope Sunflower Junction is a place you may decide to live one day."

"Um, yeah."

She didn't think Jake sounded the way she'd perceived him the other night at all. He sounded distinctly ill at ease. "Is Kitty going to show you some property?" Mary asked, to keep the silent moment from growing too long.

"I…actually, she'd mentioned me looking at yours tomorrow night."

"She did?" Mary couldn't believe it. Kitty had discouraged her from selling her house!

"Yeah. The thing is, I forgot to tell her I had my nephew staying with me. I didn't know where to call her back and make certain it was okay to bring him with me. Oh." He laughed, sounding even more uncomfortable. "She invited me to dinner. I hope she has permission to do that?"

Mary's lips parted. What in heaven's name was going on? "Well, of course you're welcome…"

There was an uncomfortable pause.

"I'm supposed to bring the chicken."

"I see." Mary frowned.

"It *is* okay, isn't it? I mentioned it was too bad you wouldn't be there when I came by to see the house and Kitty said I should stay for dinner. And that I should call you and tell you I'd bring something. Her idea sounded great at the time, but now I feel that perhaps I should have said, no, thanks."

"No, no, it's fine..."

"But...?"

Mary shifted uncomfortably in her chair. "I have to be honest, Jake. I think we're being set up. I'm used to it. She's been doing it all my life, with the best intentions, of course. Kitty is a second mom to me. To all of us. But she does tend to go overboard, whether it's making sure one of us gets the most votes for Homecoming Queen or anything else."

"Homecoming Queen?"

She heard Jake's chuckle. "Every one of us won, except Esther hasn't yet because this is only her Senior Year. Kitty would organize doughnut drives and things like that among the students to make sure they remembered our names when it was time to vote. As if there was any way there would have been a chance for anyone not to. Our graduating classes were about sixty." Mary winced. Kitty meant well, but sometimes Mary wondered if she didn't think the girls had enough of whatever it took for them to succeed on their own. Mary certainly felt as if she was a success. But now that she was beginning to see an outline to a trap laid out for Jake, she wondered.

"Well, I don't mind being set up, if that's what's bothering you."

"You don't?" She couldn't imagine any man who would like being the prize bachelor.

"No. I've been trying to get my courage up to ask you out anyway."

She was stunned.

"Listen, Mary…" he paused, and she *did* listen— with both ears straining.

"Maybe we should circumvent this plan if it bothers you. Maybe you'd like to see a movie with me tomorrow night instead?"

Her jaw dropped. She nearly lost feeling in her hand, she squeezed the phone so tightly. "I'd like that."

"You would?"

She frowned at his uncertainty. "Of course. Why not?"

"Well, you're the other victim in Kitty's scheme. It's not just me who's being set up. I have to assume that you're innocent in this. Maybe you wouldn't want to go out with me."

She heard some scuffling in the background, and a crash which sounded like something breaking. Jake covered the phone with his hand, and she wondered if she heard a muffled curse.

"I think I would like to go out with you." She kept her voice even, not too deliriously excited.

"I'll pick you up around—seven then?" he asked, speaking swiftly.

"That would be fine."

"Maybe you shouldn't mention that we're sneaking off. Keep the element of surprise in the moment."

It seemed so cruel to thwart Kitty that way! "But

what about her plan? Kitty will be so disappointed if...we don't fall in with her set-up.''

"Oh, I'll still pick up a bucket of chicken and bring it with me.''

"No, I meant about her thinking she's fixing us up.''

"You're sure that's what's on her mind?''

"Well, she just finished telling me yesterday that it was too soon for me to put my house on the market. Suddenly, it's the excuse to get you out here. Are you really interested in buying our house?''

"I'm not sure. It's definitely a consideration. It's nice," he said hastily, "but as I told Kitty, it's probably bigger than what I need. But I didn't mind coming out to see it if you were going to be around.''

Her breath tightened in her throat. Could he really mean that? "Kitty will be too thrilled to believe that she's gotten her way and hooked us up. We'll never hear the end of it.''

He chuckled. "Then definitely don't tell anyone we're going out. We'll just head out together.''

Mary couldn't help smiling as she imagined Kitty's expression when they left the house. "Okay.''

"I'll have my nephew with me, so be prepared. I hate to do that on our first date, but he just arrived. It's too soon for me to leave him with anyone.''

"Esther would love to baby-sit," Mary suggested. "Not that I mind him coming along.''

"Not this child, she wouldn't.''

"Oh, she would! Esther loves kids. And there are five other sisters and four adults for back-up.''

Something sounded like shoes hitting a wall as Jake said, "I think Cruise had better stay with me.''

"That's fine. We'll have a great time."

"Great. See you tomorrow."

The phone line disconnected. Mary turned the receiver toward her to stare at it in shock. Jake Maddox asking her out on a date? It was almost as exciting—and disturbing—as Rachel riding off on a motorcycle! Almost as fabulous as Eve's whirlwind wedding!

"It's just a date," she reminded herself sternly. "Don't be such a ninny."

Still, she felt the glow of a thousand stars inside her. She'd been invited out by a handsome man—a man whom she could tell was a good man. A guy her college friends would call a beefcake.

She, plain Mary, had her first real date in ten years! She was wanted, not needed, but *wanted* for herself—and the sensation was just short of…well, heaven.

JAKE HUNG UP THE PHONE, wincing at the shards of the priceless vase on the floor. Putting his hands on his hips, he stared Cruise down. Cruise stared back at him belligerently, then shrugged and walked away.

Jake forced himself to take deep breaths, reminding himself that Cruise was only a three-year-old child. Obviously, his rearing so far had lacked a lot. Jake had taken on this responsibility for the long haul.

But when he'd collected himself sufficiently two minutes later and tracked Cruise down in the bedroom to explain to him that breaking things was inappropriate, Jake got another shock.

Chapter Four

Cruise had taken the toothpaste out of Jake's bathroom and smeared green trails into the bedroom carpet. The room smelled like a mint garden, and the white carpet shone with slithery brilliance in large spots. Not an ounce of toothpaste lay in the nearby flattened tube. Cruise himself stared up at Jake, his hands and tennis shoes sticky with goo, waiting.

Then Cruise smiled, well-pleased with himself.

Some guilt assailed Jake as he snatched his nephew up under one arm, football-style, and carried him to his little bedroom for a spell of time-out, something he'd heard mentioned this afternoon on a parenting talk show.

He was just a child.

Jake desperately needed advice on how to raise this boy—and Mary had grown up in a family that looked like they'd known what they were doing.

Surely she could give him some pointers.

Mary wasn't likely to be interested in more than a date or two with him, a man who had never graduated from college. Not with all those diplomas with her name on them hanging on the walls.

But maybe she had a soft spot for kids.

It was too much to hope that she'd have one for both him and Cruise.

TURRIBLE TROUBLE, as Tom had predicted, made Kitty nervous. It was true she might have done a bit too much busybodying to get everything to work out according to her plan. Jake would come over tonight, he would see the newly revamped Cinderella by the name of Mary, and he would be instantly captivated.

"There's just no way this scenario fits," she muttered to Swinnie. "Mary's just too danged ornery to do what we want her to. She's got this plan, this vision for herself, and nobody's ever bothered to explain to her that sometimes the best-laid plans go to hell!"

Swinnie jumped as she burned herself on the curling iron. "You would be the expert on that."

Kitty put her hands on her hips. "What is that supposed to mean?"

"I don't know. I can hardly think you've got me so jumpy!" Swinnie cried. "I feel like I'm in the middle of a secret mission where any minute now I'm going to be discovered by double agents!"

"Oh, pooh. Get Mary in here." Kitty wasn't having any truck with such nonsense.

"Why me?"

"Because she'll suspect *me*," Kitty snapped at poor Swinnie's bewildered expression.

"Oh, all right." Swinnie went out into the hall. "Mary, dear, could you come here for just a moment?"

Mary appeared at the top of the stairs. Kitty winced

at the matronly cotton dress with the ballerina waist, ankle-length skirt. The ever-present tortoiseshell glasses were atop her nose. Her glorious hair was pulled up in a nondescript bun. "Come here, dear," she said in the sugary tone used to coax a puppy into a cage, "Swinnie and I have a surprise for you."

Mary didn't look impressed. "What kind of surprise? Aren't you two supposed to be downstairs making deviled eggs and iced tea?" That was the pretext on which her friends had gotten in the door, that certain preparations needed to be made for dinner. Mary hadn't called them on the fact that she knew Jake was bringing a bucket of chicken for dinner and there was precious little else to do. But she'd gotten busy on the Internet looking up colleges for Esther to apply to in the fall, and somehow these two had forsaken their kitchen duties.

They were up to something. She could tell it by the apple-bright shine in their eyes.

"It's just a *little* something," Kitty reassured her. "Come on in here." She ushered Mary to the powder room off the hall where it looked like a department store's worth of cosmetics and a movie star's hair equipment awaited her. "Sit right here, dear, and let your Aunt Swinnie and Aunt Kitty get to work."

Mary found herself pushed down on a vanity bench before she could say, "No thank you." Her zipper was unzipped, and she was mercilessly pulled out of her dress. A silk wrap was placed over her shoulders. Someone's hand picked at the pins in her hair, and another hand mercilessly removed her glasses. Mary wanted to argue with whatever was about to happen to her, but the crunching sound of glass forestalled her.

"Oh, dear!" Swinnie cried.

Mary whirled to see what had happened. "What was it?" she cried. "I can't see without my glasses!"

"It was nothing that a trip to the mall won't solve, dear. Don't you worry about a thing," Kitty assured her, turning her back around to face the blurry image in the mirror. "Don't you worry about a thing."

JAKE TUGGED CRUISE ALONG, one hand firmly around his nephew's wrist and one arm tucking the bucket of fried chicken carefully away from Cruise's swinging arms. The boy had not wanted to leave Jake's house, had not wanted to get into his Mercedes, did not want to go to a movie.

The only thing Cruise seemed to want to do was destroy anything in his path. Like a miniature whirlwind, his next target was unpredictable. Just as Jake thought he had the house child-proofed, Cruise tried flushing a roll of toilet paper down the toilet—fortunately, the roll was too big to get stuck. Jake gritted his teeth, doubting the wisdom of asking Mary out on a date at this point.

It was selfish of him, because Cruise wasn't going to behave. That wasn't fair to Mary, who deserved to have the kind of evening out that Jake wanted to give her. He'd used the excuse that he needed some tips on raising a child—but now he knew that the situation was way beyond helpful hints.

Ringing the doorbell, Jake waited, his stomach in a knot. He was fairly certain the evening would be a disaster.

"KEEP MARY UPSTAIRS," Kitty commanded as the doorbell sounded. She was sure her blood pressure went up a good ten points. "We'll let the boys open the door. Or one of the sisters."

"Why can't I open the door?" Mary called from her bedroom where Swinnie was spraying her with something that smelled like it might attract bees. For heaven's sake, she felt as if she were being prepared for market.

"Because you need to wait up here, dear," Kitty called back. "You mustn't appear too eager! A man likes to be kept waiting. It's part of the chase, the element of pursuit!"

Mary frowned. In her family's business, they never kept the customers waiting, neither the bed-and-breakfast vacationers nor the people who came to buy sunflowers. That had been her parent's number-one unbreakable rule: Never keep the customer waiting.

It didn't feel right going against something her parents had believed so strongly. Yet, Kitty appeared to have the bit in her teeth, and once that happened, there was no pulling back. So Mary waited, enduring Swinnie's tugs at her neckline. Mary was fairly certain that if Swinnie didn't stop, some of her cleavage was going to show. She turned toward the mirror, but that didn't help. The image was fuzzy; all she could see was the big spot of red that was her.

"I need my glasses to fully appreciate what you've done for me," she pleaded to Swinnie.

"Oh, dear. I'm embarrassed to admit that I accidentally stepped on them." Swinnie's voice was full of honest distress. "You know how nervous I get when Kitty's in the midst of one of her schemes."

She patted Mary's bare shoulders soothingly. "I'm so sorry. I will buy you another pair, dear."

Mary caught Swinnie's trembling hand in hers. "What scheme is Miss Kitty working on tonight?"

"She's just determined to catch you a...oh, Mary, you mustn't ask me!" Swinnie halted in the midst of her nervous confession.

It was just as she'd expected. With best intentions, her friends had gussied her up to catch Jake Maddox's eye. There was no reason to do so. She had a plan. And she had to stick by her plan, particularly if she was to continue overseeing the family's needs for which she was responsible. That didn't mean she didn't feel a twinge of anticipation for Jake. It certainly didn't mean she wouldn't like him to think she was pretty! But now she was all done up in a fancy dress that had some kind of stiff skirt sticking out from it, and shoes that were higher than she was used to, and her hair was up in some kind of elaborate Kitty-do, and she couldn't see a darn thing because she didn't have her glasses on. Darn it, her lips had enough gloss on them to glow in the dark.

She appreciated their efforts. But if a man was going to like her, she wanted him to like her for herself. Plain old, good-hearted Mary. Not every man was attracted to this kind of packaging.

"I'm taking this off," she announced with determination.

"Swinnie, bring Mary down, please!" Kitty called up the stairs.

"Oh, no, you mustn't do that, dear." Swinnie pried Mary's fingers off the zipper of her dress. "Come on. Jake is waiting. We don't want to keep a man waiting too long, you know. There's a world of difference between appearing too eager and appearing indifferent!''

Mary sighed to herself. While she certainly wasn't indifferent to Jake, she wasn't sure about the outcome of this pretend glamor. She sneezed, realizing it was too late to back out now. And Jake had been warned about a matchmaking attempt. Hopefully, he'd take one look at her and realize she hadn't had anything to do with this.

The last thing she wanted was for him to think she was pursuing him.

JAKE'S MOUTH DROPPED OPEN as Swinnie helped Mary down the stairs. He could tell Swinnie was helping her because Mary clutched Swinnie's arm.

"Mary, you look wonderful!" He reached up and took Mary's hand to help her the rest of the way down the stairs.

Tom and Bert had come in from the TV room to see the transformation. They stood off to the side with Kitty and Swinnie, all four beaming like sunshine.

He could tell Mary was truly uncomfortable. But he had to admit, Kitty's full-scale assault on his masculinity was definitely working. "If this is all for me," he said with conviction, "all I can say is thank you."

Mary blushed, but he thought she looked pleased— and surprised. Swinnie and Kitty, of course, just looked like they had pulled off a major coup on the enemy.

"Thanks, Jake," Mary murmured. "Let's all go

into the kitchen to eat. I don't know how long I can stand being an object of admiration."

He took her by the arm and escorted her around the stairwell to the kitchen. She smelled wonderful, like flowers in springtime. Her blond hair shone, woven in a pretty, elegant upsweep. The ladies had made her up, but not too much...and somebody had found a sexy red number that flared out from her waist to above her knees. It was the most of Mary's legs he'd seen. The top of the dress had no sleeves, and it hugged her waist and bosom like a snug triangle of material—he could honestly say he would never have envisioned such a dress on Mary.

A surge of heat ran through him. He'd come out to Sunflower Acres for many reasons, but not necessarily to fall under Mary's spell. If she'd acted like his socialite mother, smug in her glamour, he wouldn't have found her attractive. But Mary's charm lay in her innocence, and he found himself fighting the spell of attraction he hadn't counted on.

MARY HEARD the change in Jake's voice. It worried her. She was determined to be liked just for herself! Whatever Kitty and Swinnie had done for her, it was obviously as successful as any of the blue-ribbon confections they'd ever cooked up for the State Fair, because Jake sounded like he couldn't believe his eyes.

On the other hand, his unexpected admiration sort of made her shivery with pleasure.

"Don't like her," a small voice announced from somewhere near her elbow.

CRUISE GIBSON MADDOX knew one thing as he stared up at the tall woman who had his uncle's complete attention. She reminded him of his grandmother. Grandmother was always like a statue that couldn't be touched. You couldn't touch her hair, and you couldn't hug her because you might wrinkle her dress. If she kissed you, it was fast and brief and left a yucky stain on your cheek which had to be rubbed off.

This woman looked like she enjoyed Uncle Jake being around. Cruise's mother always liked to have men around, so much so that she never had time for Cruise. He had to watch a lot of TV while his mother visited. He hated TV, and he hated his mother paying attention to everyone but him.

Cruise got a lot of mileage out of misbehaving. It was the only surefire way to get an adult's attention. So far it had worked with Uncle Jake.

But now he'd let go of Cruise's hand to hold the woman's hand who wore the bright red dress—and she was smiling with shiny lips at Uncle Jake.

"Don't like her," he repeated loudly.

Chapter Five

"Why, what have we here?" Kitty swept Cruise up into her arms, much to the child's astonishment. "What a precious little moppet!" she cried, obviously intent on overlooking his awkward pronouncement. "Why, precious *and* precocious!" She smiled, staring into Cruise's eyes. "Do you know what precocious means?"

Dumbfounded and out of his league with this sudden burst of attention, he shook his head.

"It means you talk too much, sweetheart!" She gave him her sweetest grandma smile. "You can only get away with that when you're three—and then later on when you're my age. Bert, you and Tom take Cruise down to see the fish pond. Would you like to see some catfish that are as big as your arm?"

Cruise didn't move, transfixed by Kitty's enthusiasm. He wasn't quite sure if he'd lost command of the adults or not.

"Of course you would!" Kitty handed him off to the men. "You boys run on down to the pond, and I'll ring the triangle for supper just as soon as I see these young people off!" Satisfied that Cruise was departing, she turned her focus on Jake and Mary. "Now then, you two go have a wonderful time and don't worry about a thing." She smiled benignly at Jake. "We've had a hand in raising these seven sisters; we can certainly watch one little tyke for a few hours."

Jake wasn't so sure about that. The bucket of chicken was whisked from his possession. He and Mary were herded toward the front door.

"But Kitty," Mary tried to interrupt, "we invited Jake to eat chicken with us!"

"Oh, no, my dear. We invited him to bring some chicken over because y'all were going into town. Now, Jake, you take good care of my girl. Take her some place she can show off that marvelous dress, like a fancy restaurant. Not a movie, because nobody can admire her in the dark." Kitty and Swinnie beamed as they looked at Mary and Jake together. "I must say you make a handsome couple."

Jake and Mary glanced at each other, shy and a little embarrassed by Kitty's machinations.

"Well, ta-ta! Be sure to make certain Mary's buckled into your car properly, Jake! When a person isn't used to the seat belts in a car, they can be tricky!" She closed the door, and Jake found himself on the porch staring into Mary's mortified eyes.

"I'm so sorry! I had no idea she'd act this way!" Mary apologized.

"To tell you the truth, I need a moment to catch my breath," he admitted with a grin. "Your Aunt Kitty could be a corporate raider or a four-star general with all that energy."

She laughed. "Kitty could have been anything she

wanted. I believe she was happy being Mrs. Fred May.''

''No doubt that's why she's so set on finding you a mister.''

Self-conscious, she lowered her eyelashes. ''Miss Kitty is just a born organizer. Right now, I think she's intent on organizing my family.'' Mary gave him a soft smile. ''She wasn't quite this bad before my parents passed away. Oh, she ran her Homecoming Queen campaigns, and occasionally some terribly wonderful surprise would show up at our birthday parties, like a playhouse big enough for ten that was fully furnished and decorated for tea parties. But nothing as bad as trying to snare me a husband.''

''I suppose I should be flattered.'' Miss Kitty was handing him a gorgeous woman with an engraved invitation to carry her off. What male could fail to appreciate her generous gift?

Mary laughed. ''Be flattered if you like. There's no harm in Miss Kitty, and you're safe from me.''

''Am I?'' He wasn't sure he wanted to be.

Her eyes softened, but her smile stayed. ''Yes. Of course. I have a year of residency in California which starts in a few weeks. That pretty much puts me out of the serious relationship market.''

''Yeah, I suppose it does.'' He felt the sinking of his heart and knew it was disappointment. But he'd never felt an urge to spend a lot of time with one woman before! ''I haven't been much for relationship roulette myself. My company keeps me pretty busy.'' He ran a hand through his hair, wondering if it was safe to leave Cruise. What trouble would his nephew get into with elderly folk who weren't in shape to watch him? "I feel guilty leaving Cruise with your family. Do you think it's a good idea? He can be a handful." He heard himself use Steffie's word and realized now how true the adjective was.

"If you're worried, go in and wrest him away from Miss Kitty." Mary smiled at him. "I don't mind him coming with us."

He slid a glance from Mary's shiny hair to her feet. Wearing those high heels brought her nearly to his level, and he found it incredibly exciting to be this near her lips and to look into her sexy aquamarine eyes. "I think I'll enjoy Miss Kitty's manipulation and leave him, if you think your relatives are up to baby-sitting."

She ran her hand through the crook in his arm he extended. "We don't have to stay out late. But I think Cruise is in good company."

Fortunately, he could call and check on him from his cell phone. "I hope you're right," he muttered, thinking about the toothpaste incident and the swimming toilet roll.

But if time was running out, then he'd better make the most of this night. "Is there somewhere special you'd like to go?"

She gave an impatient snort. "To a mall to get my glasses prescription filled. Swinnie broke them to-night, accidentally."

"Accidentally?" Jake thought those two women were capable of anything but not "accidents." Realizing Mary really couldn't see very well, he was careful to help her down the porch steps. Walking her to the car, he helped her in.

"I do think it was an accident. This particular incident, anyway."

Jake allowed himself to take Kitty's advice and make certain Mary was securely buckled in her seat. He brushed her bare shoulders and felt fire heating inside him as he crossed her lap with the belt. "You smell nice."

"Thank you."

He heard the shyness in her tone. "Did I tell you how great you look?"

"I think so. Everything happened so fast."

She was fastened in the seat and not going anywhere. There was no need to linger this closely. But all that soft bare skin was so tempting…

Puzzlement at his hesitation showed in her eyes.

He thought if he didn't kiss her he might burst. It just had to be done.

"Just in case anything else happens too quickly tonight," he murmured, "I'll go ahead and ask you for a good-night kiss now."

"I…all right." She didn't move. "Oh! Was that the question already? I mean, did you just ask, or are you about to ask?"

"Does it matter?"

"Not especially," she murmured. "I just wanted to be prepared."

He smiled and pressed his lips to hers. Her lips parted in surprise. Lingering just a moment past what could be genuinely called a good-night kiss, Jake savored the feeling of Mary's softness and the fact that her lips molded under his with sweet compliance. He kissed her again, and then once more before he realized he couldn't do this much longer or they would never get to Dallas. Regretfully pulling away, Jake picked up Mary's hand and kissed it before setting her hand in her lap. He stood.

"Jake?"

"Yes?" He hoped she wasn't about to tell him he'd overdone it. His head was buzzing with the desire to kiss her again!

"I wasn't quite ready for that."

"You weren't?"

"No. You know how sometimes you blink when your picture's being taken and you know your eyes were closed?"

His brows rose. What was she trying to tell him? "Yeah. I've done that a time or two myself."

"Then you have to take another one to get it right. A do-over."

He grinned. "Are you saying you want a do-over?"

"I just want you to be sure you get a real goodnight kiss later, no matter what else happens tonight."

"You've got a deal." Jake walked around and got in the driver's side of the car, filled with anticipation.

"I think I wasn't ready because I can't see you properly."

"Maybe it's better that way," he said on a laugh as he pulled down the driveway.

"I don't think so. I could probably kiss better if I could see what I was doing."

"Kissing isn't exactly a seeing thing, do you think?"

"Well," she said uncertainly, "I haven't done a whole lot of studying on that subject."

He grinned. "Tell you what. Kitty and Swinnie will

probably be upset, because I don't think breaking your glasses was all that accidental. But why don't I take you to one of those one-hour shops and get you another pair?'' He sent her his best, most gentlemanly grin, but he couldn't help the mischief in his tone. "Then we could study kissing all you like.''

She pursed her lips at his teasing. "Why do I have the feeling you've gotten an *A* in that subject before?''

He didn't reply. To be honest, there weren't many subjects he'd ever gotten a good grade in. Sooner or later he was going to have to tell Mary about his lack of education. It was difficult to admit with her interest in academics.

But if Mary van Doorn would let him kiss her again tonight, he'd put enough effort into *that* to get an *A++*.

"DID YOU SEE THAT?'' Kitty crowed triumphantly as the Mercedes pulled down the drive. She and Swinnie had been spying through the curtain panel, and it was obvious that all their hard work had not gone for naught.

"He kissed her!'' Swinnie cried. They high-fived each other. "Won't Bert and Tom be amazed!''

"Oh, my gosh! I forgot they were down at the pond with that little troublemaker!'' Kitty ran to ring the triangle.

"Should you call him that?'' Swinnie wasn't certain that was appropriate. Cruise was Jake's nephew, after all.

"Just once I can,'' Kitty assured her. "He could have ruined their evening with his little opinion,

which he can just keep to himself in the future!"
Swiftly, she laid out the chicken and rolls. "Fortunately, rather than dwelling on it, our man had enough sense to plant one on Mary."

"It was quite a kiss," Swinnie agreed. "Many seconds past your average, garden-variety peck."

"Oh, way past that. I would say he was closer to testing the waters."

Swinnie looked over her silver spectacles. "Testing for what?"

Kitty glanced up. "Well, you know. To see if he liked her. If he's attracted to her."

"Well, he'd be a fool not to be with her in that dress."

"Red satin will do it every time," Kitty said with satisfaction. "Mercy! What happened to you three?"

Bert, Tom and Cruise stood at the back door, covered to their ears in mud and pond grass.

Cruise was wearing a devilish grin.

"If those catfish aren't dead of a heart attack by morning," Bert said dolefully, "I'm positive *I* will be!"

MARY SIGHED with absolute happiness as she slid her glasses onto her face. These frames were lighter, and gold in tone. She was so used to her more sturdy tortoiseshell frames she was interested to see how they'd feel. "Oh, that's so much better!" Smiling at the technician, she turned to thank Jake.

Her eyes widened. "Don't you look nice?" she said warmly, her gaze roving every inch of him, seeing things she'd been unable to see before. He had such blue eyes! Deep, deep blue—and they were sparkling at her. Nice firm lips—she'd barely allowed herself to notice them before, but now that he'd kissed her, she looked more intently.

His khaki pants were nicely pressed. A shirt of navy blue with a soft weave clung to a nicely muscled frame. "Goodness, I can't believe you kissed me," she murmured. Why would a man as handsome as Jake Maddox be interested in her?

He kissed her again, right there in front of the technician. "Were you ready that time?" he asked.

"No!" She hadn't been. He'd caught her totally off guard. It felt reckless and spontaneous and wonderful. "You'll have to give me another chance."

Chuckling, he took her by the elbow and led her from the store. "I'm supposed to take you to a fancy restaurant to show you off. Kitty's orders. I can't get sidetracked by kissing you, much as I'd like to."

She sighed. "And I'm not supposed to be wearing glasses." Sliding them into the case, she put them in the small red-satin clutch Kitty had given her. "But I sincerely appreciate you bringing me to get new ones. I wouldn't have been able to look over the accounts tomorrow."

"Glad to do it." They were quiet as they walked through the mall toward the car. "You're not going to sell, are you? I'm just wondering since you're leaving to do your residency."

"Are you interested?"

His gaze ran along her curves with blatant male enthusiasm. "Yes."

"In the property!" She gave him a light smack on the arm, but reveled in his two-sided answer.

"No. I'm only curious."

She shrugged. "I haven't thought through what I'm going to do yet. With all the sisters going one way or another, it just leaves me and Esther. And we'll be in California. I guess." She felt guilty about Esther's senior year. How nice it had been to live in Sunflower Junction, enjoying a year of hometown friends and parties! But she couldn't leave Esther in the house alone. "It's hard to believe Eve will be married in two weeks," she said.

"Could you rent the house out for a year?"

"I could, I suppose. I hadn't thought of that. Frankly, starting a practice is so iffy. I don't think starting one in Sunflower Junction where the population is under twenty would help me pay back my college loans. So there isn't much reason to hang on to Sunflower Acres."

He wanted to sneak his hand up under that stiff, sexy bell-shaped skirt and trace her thighs. And maybe her bottom, too. Jake sighed, the errant fantasy striking him from out of nowhere.

Heaven save him from well-meaning older ladies and beautiful women who already had their goals in sight. Mary was deadly serious about leaving Texas— and him—behind. He might never get her out of that dress.

Mary patted his arm, smiling up at him when he sighed.

"Tired?" she asked.

He shook his head. He would never be tired of being with her. "I was just thinking about Cruise."

"Don't worry. I'm sure he's having a great time."

Jake snorted and pulled Mary a little closer to him. "I think I'll call your house if you don't mind."

She sat down on a bench. "Go right ahead."

He sat down next to her. After he punched in the numbers she gave him, he reached for Mary's hand. They sat there companionably until someone picked up at the other end.

"Hello?"

"Kitty?" Jake asked.

"Oh, hello, dear. Yes, it's me!" Kitty said happily. "Are you two having a wonderful time? How's my Mary?"

"She's fine, and yes, we're having a good time." He smiled as Mary lightly squeezed his fingers in agreement. "Is Cruise giving you a run for your money?"

"Oh, no. We're having such fun. He's been swimming, and we're about to water the garden and then have a picnic!"

Jake breathed a sigh of relief. "I'm so glad he's behaving."

"Don't you worry about a thing," Kitty assured him. "You just take good care of my girl!"

"I will. Bye." Jake turned the phone off and slid it into his pocket. "They seem to be doing fine."

She laid her head on his shoulder, and Jake thought nothing had ever felt as good as Mary being close to him.

"I told you. Miss Kitty can handle just about anything."

"They went swimming, and now they're about to picnic."

Mary sat up. "Hmm. We don't have a swimming pool."

Jake frowned. "I could have sworn she said Cruise

had been swimming. And now they're about to water the garden. And then picnic.''

Mary considered his words before shaking her head in resignation. ''Oh, well. Kitty's got the heart of a child. Who knows what she's up to?'' Her eyes shaded with distress. ''I do wish Cruise hadn't decided he didn't like me.''

''Cruise is going through a lot right now. I wouldn't worry about it too much.''

Jake pressed Mary's head back against his shoulder. Cruise's instant dislike of Mary worried him, too. But as they had just discussed, Cruise need not worry about them becoming a three-member family.

At least he was enjoying an evening at Sunflower Acres, and that hopefully would get the ball rolling in the right direction. Jake wanted Cruise to be happy, and to become a well-adjusted little boy. Maybe a way to help that along was to spend time with people who were normal and kind.

''STAND STILL!'' Kitty instructed Tom, Bert and Cruise. She picked up the hose, and waved at Swinnie to turn it on. ''How two grown men can't keep one little boy out of the fish pond I'll never know, but this is the only way I can think of to clean you up.'' She gave Tom and Bert her most exasperated look. ''Honestly!''

Water ran out of the hose and Kitty carefully washed Cruise first. When the mud was out of his hair and ears and the creases of his neck, she allowed Swinnie to envelop the boy in a nice dry towel.

Then she turned the hose full blast on her two cronies.

"Hey! Take it easy, Kitty!" Bert cried.

Cruise giggled at the two grown men hopping from one foot to the other as Kitty sprayed them mercilessly.

"What do you think, Cruise? You were much more grown up about your bath than they are."

"You didn't have the spray nozzle on the hose when you cleaned him up. It stings, Kitty!" Bert hollered.

"You have more creases and wrinkles than Cruise does," she asserted, giving a good brisk spraying to both their backsides, which were turned toward her in self-defense. "It requires more drastic measures to clean you up."

Finally, she was satisfied that she had extracted enough punishment. Turning the water off, she glared at the two barefoot men with their soggy jeans rolled up over their ankles. "If you two aren't a sight."

"Don't we get a nice soft towel to dry off with?" Tom asked hopefully, his gaze darting Swinnie's way for pity.

"Nope. Run around the back forty. You'll be dry in a jiff," Kitty informed them, rolling up the hose. She swept her palms off. "Now if you two think you can keep out of trouble for the short time it takes me to go in and get the chicken, we'll have a picnic on the patio."

She raised an eyebrow at the grown men, and winked at Cruise.

"Yes, Kitty." Tom and Bert said in unison, but they slid a wary look Cruise's way.

"Don't try to blame this on him," she said with a jerk of her head at the little boy. "If he had been properly supervised, you wouldn't be standing there with your drawers dripping.''

They sent her their best glares.

Kitty turned and marched inside. Swinnie was pouring tea into plastic glasses painted with orange and yellow sunflowers.

''Don't you think you were just a teeny bit hard on Tom and Bert?'' Swinnie asked as she set the pitcher down.

''Maybe, but it sure was fun watching them jump around!''

''Oh, Kitty,'' Swinnie said, shaking her head as she giggled. Wiping her eyes with the corner of her apron, she wondered, ''Whatever would we do without you for entertainment?''

''Not a darn thing,'' Kitty asserted. ''You'd be stuck watching 'The Price Is Right' with Tom and Bert for the rest of your life.'' But as she carried a platter outside, Swinnie's question ran through her mind once more.

And sparked an idea.

Chapter Six

Mary was having the time of her life. For a woman who had never known romance, she was getting a heavenly helping of it tonight. Jake held her hand in his big strong one as they walked along a cobbled path after enjoying a moonlight dinner in downtown Dallas. The city lights sparkled with dizzyingly happy effervescence, a nice light breeze teased the hem of her flippy short skirt, and Jake's eyes held admiration every time she met his gaze.

She wished tonight would never end. All her cares were washing away in the star-sprinkled night.

When Jake slid his hand up her arm to cup her shoulder and pull her close to him, Mary sighed with the nerve-tingling wonder of it all. He was about the sexiest man she had ever laid eyes on. Who would have ever thought Mary van Doorn could be living this dream?

"As much as I hate to do this, I'm going to have to take you home," Jake said, his voice deep with regret. "I feel guilty leaving Cruise with your family this long."

"I understand. It hasn't been an imposition. But it is getting late."

Jake had to go to work tomorrow, and she had accounts to decipher. There were so many things she didn't know about running Sunflower Acres. Her parents had kept everything running with clockwork precision for so long that she had taken that smoothness for granted, believing it was how life was. Now there were bills she had to pay for equipment repair and irrigation, supplies she had to order, and a constant stream of phone calls from people who wanted to stay at the famous bed and breakfast. Those calls she felt guilty about turning down. She and her sisters weren't equipped to run that part of the business right now. She was barely hanging on to the floral end of it, down to telling people to come out and roam the fields cutting what they liked for a set fee. It kept the blooms from wasting, and meant Mary didn't have as much work to do.

But it wasn't the way her parents had done things. They would be appalled at her lack of organization. Yet it was difficult, almost suffocating with the responsibilities and demands she had to learn in such a short while!

"You were smiling, and now you're not." Jake gave her a squeeze which brought Mary back to the moment. "I'm only taking you home because I'm afraid Cruise is tearing up your house and wearing out your family. If I had my way, I'd keep you out until the sun comes up."

She smiled. "It's not that. I've got to get home anyway."

"Six sisters keep you busy?"

Mary leaned into his palm as it glided along her cheek. "Well, between helping Eve plan her wedding, and wondering if I should have discouraged Rachel from going off, and worrying about the rest of the girls, sometimes it feels a bit overwhelming."

"Half a dozen siblings is a lot. Hey, I'm worn out by Cruise and he's just one kid."

Mary glanced up at Jake. "I would guess that one three-year-old boy more than equals six grown sisters for energy."

He laughed. "I tell myself it's good practice for the future, though. One day I'll have my own children, and I'll be glad Cruise ran me through a few of the ropes."

Mary's skin felt suddenly chilled. Jake wanted children. Of course he did. And he'd be the kind of man willing to put the time commitment in, rather than father the kids and hand them off to the wife.

Mary couldn't envision children in her future for a very long time. She thought it best to simply nod.

"One of the reasons I sympathize with Cruise so much is that I know how lonely it is to be an only child. My sister and I were so many years apart that we were essentially only kids. We had different fathers. Our mother was intent on her social climb, and after my dad died and left her a fortune, she was determined to find another rich husband. Which she did. Rich husbands led to rich pursuits, but not much family time. Steffie grew up needing attention. She didn't get it, so I guess she found a boyfriend to give her that attention."

His eyes turned hard with unpleasant memories. "My sister's teenage pregnancy was more than

Mother could bear. It would look bad to her society friends. So she tried everything to get Steffie to give Cruise up for adoption. Realizing she had Mother's attention at last, Steffie wasn't about to give in.''

He shrugged, as if the bitterness didn't eat at him anymore, but Mary saw through the brave façade. She squeezed his hand.

''I don't see why one little boy has to be a pawn, a forgotten, unloved child just because he was born into bad circumstances. I can't allow my nephew to grow up thinking he's done something wrong.''

She'd taken her family's love and closeness for granted, Mary realized. By the deeply haunted shadow in Jake's eyes, she knew he had never known any of the security she'd known. He identified with Cruise and Steffie because he'd lived that same way: ignored and unwanted. A burden.

He wanted a family. He wanted what he'd never had, and what he was determined to make certain Cruise didn't miss out on. It was something he dreamed of as much as she dreamed of becoming a doctor. His dream was a need. An intense hunger.

The last thing she could handle right now was more obligations and responsibilities. But she understood the importance of a dream.

''I'm just not ready for the night to end, I guess. Would you go on a carriage ride with me?'' At her nod, Jake paid for a ride in a horse-drawn carriage and helped her into the seat. He settled next to her with a wry expression.

''I'm only telling you this because I want you to know who I am.'' He ran his palm down her arm in a slow sensual movement that electrified her skin as he clasped her hand in his. "I know Kitty and crew see me as a bachelor who's marriage material, but I'm lacking the résumé they want for you." He smiled, self-deprecatingly. "One troubled little boy. No college education. That's what I've got to offer. The opportunity to date a man with a high-school diploma and spend time with a three-year-old."

"Jake!" Mary couldn't stand to hear him talk like that. "I'm sure Kitty picked out a man who she believed had honor and decency! She's not shallow enough to be concerned about the things you mention. For that matter, neither am I." Gently, she squeezed his hand. "I've never liked men who thought they had to impress me with their brains just because I had more education than they did." She gazed into his eyes. "I want to be wanted. I want a man to think about my heart and my soul, not discuss organic and chemical compounds with me." Her eyelids lowered. "And whether or not you have Cruise to raise makes no difference to me. I don't assume you're looking for a stepmother for him, and you shouldn't assume that he's a problem to me."

He kissed her hand. "I'm sorry," he murmured. "I just wanted you to know who I am. Just in case Kitty and crew had misread my credentials."

"I'm not shopping for a man," Mary assured him. "I wouldn't compare résumés, and you don't know me very well if you think I'd let Kitty or anyone else pick out my future husband."

His gaze measured her, assessing her words. "They *have* conspired to get us together."

"Yes, they have. But *I* let them!"

He grinned at her.

"Is there something wrong with admitting that I like you? That I find it flattering that a man like you would want to go out with a woman like me?" she demanded.

"What do you mean by 'a woman like you'?" He frowned at her.

"Well, I'm not exactly the kind of woman you no doubt meet in Dallas," she said with some heat. "I'm not beautiful, and up-to-date on the latest fashions. Kitty and Swinnie got this outfit together for me—" she said with a sweep of her hand toward the flared skirt "—and I can assure you I own nothing like this."

"It's very attractive on you," he murmured. "You sure took my breath away."

"I know you mean that to be a compliment, but the truth is," Mary said, "if I was looking for a man, *and I'm not,* I'd find one who liked me for *me.* Ankle-length dresses and all!" she exclaimed, her hands holding the skirt at each edge for emphasis.

Jake's eyes widened as he took in the fact that Mary's outraged handling of her red-satin skirt had raised the hem two inches. Much higher and he was going to drag her to his house to remove it from her lusciously full-figured body.

"I liked your other dress just fine," he said swiftly to placate her. "I like you just for you."

"You don't!" Mary smoothed the skirt down to his relief. She crossed her arms belligerently, which made her breasts mold roundly and rise up over the straight neckline of the wedge-shaped top. He felt like he was about to break a sweat in the suddenly too-hot evening air. "You wouldn't be staring at me like a wolf if I wasn't in this dress."

He tried very hard not to smile at her concern. "I thought you wanted to be wanted, like any other woman," he pointed out reasonably.

"I do! But I just think you should know that this is a borrowed dress!"

Mary's eyes glowed turquoise in the dim light from the street lamps. Her hair had loosened a little during the carriage ride, giving her a very sexy, slightly tousled look. He hated to tell her, but he didn't care about the dress. She was tall and beautiful, she had everything he was looking for, and he wanted to kiss her this second under the street lamps lighting the night.

"Mary van Doorn," he said huskily, "you're beautiful."

Her lips parted in amazement. "Nobody's ever said that to me before."

"Mary van Doorn, you're beautiful," he repeated, moving close to draw her into his arms. "And I hope you're ready this time, because it's your last chance to get prepared for the kiss I've been wanting to give you all evening."

He kissed her until Mary could feel shivers running all over her. He kissed her until she thought her heart would beat right out of her chest. Mary van Doorn held onto Jake's muscular frame for dear life, sighing with sheer delight at the sensation of being wanted by this man. A passerby in another carriage whistled, but Mary didn't care. She closed her eyes and gloried in Jake's hands pressing her more tightly to him.

When he finally moved his head back to gaze down

at her, Mary stared up at him through emotion-heavy eyes.

"Were you ready for that?" he asked.

Mary's lips curved in a soft, satisfied smile. "Yes."

He chuckled. "I'm not so sure I was."

So he'd felt the same crazy tipping of the earth that she had. Mary loved knowing that she affected him like that.

"Results should always be quantified and duplicated to verify that the data is reliable," she murmured. "Do it again, Jake."

"WE WEREN'T having an argument, you know," Mary assured Jake as he helped her into his car ten minutes later. After he'd kissed her breathless again— as she'd encouraged him to do—they'd walked in contented, yet aware-of-each-other silence back to the car. Suddenly, she'd remembered what he had said about his mother and sister, and how they hadn't been close. She wondered if his family had bickered a lot. He didn't seem to like them very much.

He walked around to the driver's side and slid in, sending her a teasing look. "We most certainly weren't."

He was referring to the amount of kissing they'd done. She felt a flush and a tingle run over her skin. "I don't want you to think I'm difficult to get along with."

That made him chuckle as he started the car. "Now, what would make me think that?"

"Well," Mary said, "all this talk about qualifications made me wonder if Kitty had mentioned any of mine to you."

"Actually, no."

"So she just sneaked me up on you? Without describing my assets as if I were one of her properties?"

Jake scratched the back of his neck. "I think so. One minute I was looking for real estate, a place to raise Cruise that wasn't knee-deep in urban problems, and the next minute, Kitty was introducing me to you. We haven't had a discussion about real estate since."

Mary nodded as if that made sense. "She's going to keep finding ways to throw us together if we're not careful."

He wasn't sure he liked her meaning. "Shouldn't we like being thrown together?" Certainly, he liked being with Mary. He hoped she liked being with him.

"Yes, but only in situations of our own making." With wide, clear eyes that had surely picked apart many an equation, Mary gazed at him. "Don't you see? We're the victims of good intentions. And it has made us argue."

"I'm not sure I follow." Maybe that was because he had one eye on the road and one on Mary's smooth thigh which showed beneath the edge of the shiny red material.

"The reason Kitty and crew like to do so much for me is because they think I can't do it by myself."

Jake frowned. "I don't think that's why they do anything at all."

"Oh, yes, it is. Instead of Calamity Jane, I'm more like Misfortune Mary in their eyes. They have always paved the way for me."

"They do it because they love you."

"Yes."

Mary nodded emphatically, and one of the pins fell out of her hair. It was beginning to loosen in the most intriguing manner. Jake supposed he wasn't much of a gentleman to allow his thoughts to go where they were going, but how could he concentrate on anything when her soft hair was bouncing against her bare skin? It made him want to touch her softness in the worst way.

"And like any good parents, they want the best for me. Just like you do for Cruise."

"Of course."

"It's only natural."

"I agree. So what's the problem?" He didn't see that there was a problem, except that Mary was talking theorems when she should be talking romance.

"The problem is that they take matters into their own hands!" Mary clarified. "We would never have had heated words tonight if we hadn't been thrown together. We each felt like we had something about ourselves that might be undesirable to the other person, so we revealed those things. Perhaps before we were ready. And it made us uncomfortable."

"Lady, I gotta tell you, I don't find a whole heck of a lot of anything undesirable about you." Jake thought it was time he cleared that up.

"Well, I—" That seemed to startle her for a moment. Then she caught a second wave of enthusiasm for her topic. "We wouldn't have felt concerned if we'd found each other the usual way, without being manipulated into being together."

"Who cares how it happened? I'm having a great time." Jake slid a hand over to her thigh, caressing the soft skin appreciatively. "And I didn't think our words got all that heated, anyway."

"I just want to do things for myself," Mary said. "I don't want to be looked after and helped along forever. I must sound terribly ungrateful to you, ungrateful for all of this. When I was a child, playhouses and Homecoming Queen crowns appearing out of thin air at Kitty's behest were little-girl dreams come true." She looked up at Jake with her heart in her eyes. "But now I'm a big girl. I want the things that I'm going to have to come of my own making."

"You earned your medical degree on your own."

She nodded, knowing that he was beginning to understand.

"But you want a man who hasn't been hand-picked for you." He turned the car smoothly toward the highway. "Someone who likes you whether you're wearing a hellaciously sexy red dress or a grungy sack. No Kitty and crew magic."

She beamed. "Precisely."

"Does Kitty know this?" He sent her a sideways look, one eyebrow raised in curiosity.

"No," she said softly, her heart aching. "But I plan on telling her very soon." She liked Jake, liked him very much. But she knew Kitty too well. There was no way she'd quit now that she'd selected a man for Mary. Jake and Mary would be walking down the aisle if Kitty had her way.

But Mary didn't intend to see Jake any more.

"HERE'S THE PLAN," Kitty announced. She gave each of her conspirators a sharp eyeing to make certain they were paying attention. "Did I ever tell you

you're a ragged lot?'' she asked Tom and Bert, whose wind-dried clothes were mud-spattered from their unexpected swim.

Bert jumped at her criticism. "You'd look mighty ragged too if you'd been chasing a little boy all night!"

"How is one little boy different from seven girls?" she demanded with asperity.

It hadn't been, and she knew Bert couldn't argue with that. The van Doorn girls possessed plenty of high spirits, and it had taken nearly the entire community to keep up with their comings and goings. Not many weeks had gone by that the girls weren't mentioned in the *Sunflower Junction Chronicle.* There were days the *Chronicle* read more like a gossip column than a small-town newspaper. Some weeks the girls were mentioned for good grades; sometimes it was because they'd painted their graduation year on the town water tower or some equally mischievous antic. Kitty had nearly aged to a full head of white hair over those stunts. Every time she thought about those girls climbing up that yellow-and-white water tower in the middle of the night to paint each of their graduating years in bright blue paint, she felt a tightening in her chest.

The year the twins had graduated, it had been two of the girls scaling, armed with spray paint.

It was tradition, the girls explained every time it happened. The graduating year had to be celebrated in this manner. Ever since Mary had begun the tradition, the van Doorn girls had always been elected by their classmates to do the honors.

Most likely it was because with only one or two

siblings in other families, their parents didn't want to waste a child by allowing them to fall off the water tower, Kitty sniffed to herself. The van Doorns would still have half a dozen if one of theirs got seriously hurt.

That was one blot in her plans. This would be Esther's graduating year—the last class to go through Sunflower Junction's high school, unless the town grew again, which didn't seem likely. If Kitty achieved her goal and married Mary off, then Esther would be here to graduate.

And Esther was an artist. Extremely gifted with paintbrushes, charcoal, whatever she could lay hands on.

But Esther, the baby, would *not* be climbing that water tower to showcase her talent. Such an event would only happen over Kitty's dead body. She would find a way to circumvent the youngest van Doorn from such a foolhardy act.

Who would have ever thought that lady-like, sweet, non-hooligan Mary could have been coerced into such a reckless deed in the first place? It had started an unfortunate, unnecessary cycle of repetitious reckless behavior amongst her sisters. But Kitty was determined that the cycle be broken with Esther, the baby.

"So what's cooking under that gray-haired mop of yours?" Tom inquired. "You look like you're still putting the pieces together."

Kitty snapped out of her reminiscing and lasered him with a glare to show him that she was in full control of the situation. "I haven't yet sold Jake a property, but I believe from his attendance on Mary, we can assume that he is fairly interested in the area. For Cruise's sake,'' she amended.

The boy was asleep, bless him, tuckered out from playing with four old folks. His swim in the pond had been wearying to his dear little muscles, and his exercise after supper had consisted of playing hide and seek with Bert and Tom. Then Kitty had put him in some of the girls' old clothes, which had brought back fond, bittersweet memories of little, blond-haired cherubic girls running around the farm in blue-jean shorts and T-shirts.

My, but they had been hellions.

Then she'd given Cruise a mug of warm milk and read him *The Gingerbread Man,* which he'd thoroughly enjoyed because of the misbehavior on the part of the cookie. She suspected he hadn't been read to very often as he'd pleaded for her to read the book three times. Finally, tuckered out, warm and comfortable, he'd fallen asleep in her lap.

Just like the old days, she had thought wistfully.

It was time to engage her plan at mach speed. Mary was too danged slow in seeing what an advantageous opportunity she had in Jake. He would make a good husband. She would make a good wife and stepmother.

They would make lots of babies for Kitty, Swinnie, Tom and Bert. Maybe another seven!

''Okay, so Jake likes the area, and you'll sell him a house. So what?'' Bert demanded.

''Let me get you a glass of milk and a cookie,'' she told him. ''You're getting fussy.''

''Yes, I am. I missed 'The Price Is Right,' and I'm exhausted from baby-sitting,'' he complained. ''I'm supposed to be retired, and enjoying the easy-chair days of my life.''

Kitty snorted. She'd seen him hiding behind the trunk of a live oak tree until Cruise had nearly backed up to him in his ''seeking.'' Bert had reached out with a small tree limb and given Cruise a little tickle on the back of his neck, just enough to make him think some spidery critter had jumped on him. Once he jerked around and saw it was just Bert, he'd giggled and run after him.

Bert could still pick up his boots to a fast pace, so Kitty ignored his complaint. She dished out a cookie to everyone and set it beside a glass of milk. ''The so-what is that I think Jake will eventually ask Mary to be his wife.''

''We haven't got *eventually*,'' Tom reminded her crustily. ''And no man proposes in two weeks. Unless he's really ripe for the pickin' like Eve's fiancé or Rachel's.''

''Jake strikes me as opportunely ripe,'' Swinnie mused.

''All right then.'' Bert leaned back in his chair expansively. ''So maybe you sell him a house, and maybe Jake asks Mary to marry him. Is that the end of it, the trophy, the blue ribbon? And we can get back to resting?''

''Well, there'll be Cruise then, I suspect. He'll give us considerable to do.''

Bert and Tom groaned, but Kitty ignored them. ''We'll have to start thinking about opening Junction's elementary when he's of the age for schooling. There'll be other babies to follow, if Mary gets cracking.'' She smiled in anticipation.

"But Mary wants to be a doctor!" Bert pounded his fist on the table.

"She can be a doctor here!" Kitty insisted. "Why should I not get the benefit of her raising? Just because I'm in good health doesn't mean I'm going to be this way when I'm one hundred! Mary might as well be doctoring us as anybody else in the country."

"But she's got that year of residency," Bert said dolefully.

"There is that." Swinnie bit her cookie, and drank some milk. "It won't take us a whole year to clean out the old doc's clinic while we wait for her."

"No, and I don't reckon Jake will go for his woman taking off for a year." That was another blot she couldn't see past. Mary's most certain departure for at least a year, and the fact that Esther, the baby, would no doubt feel compelled to ascend the water tower to honor the family name and school tradition.

"Everyone agrees that speed is of the utmost necessity?" Kitty asked, glancing around the table.

There were three uncertain nods, as if no one was sure exactly what they were seconding.

"Then I will sell Jake a property."

"Which one?" Bert wanted to know.

"I haven't thought that far ahead." She peeked over a sofa at Cruise, who slept peacefully despite their voices. Whatever she sold his uncle, it had to be a nice place for an energetic tot to play. "Sunflower Acres would be good, except that Mary's not selling. Well, she thinks she is, but I've discouraged her from that rash idea."

"Of course if Jake buys it, then Mary's already

here, and shoot, they might as well just move in together!'' Swinnie exclaimed.

"There'll be no moving in together.'' Kitty didn't
like the sound of that at all. "He signs the marriage
certificate *before* he signs the deed. Not one cereal
bowl moves in here until he does so.''

They all digested the "plan'' in thoughtful silence.

The door opened, startling them into guilty jumps.

"Mary!'' Kitty exclaimed. "What are you doing
home so early?''

Mary closed the door behind her and Jake. "We
both have to work tomorrow. But we had a wonderful
time.''

Kitty was happy to note the smiles that passed between the two. "I'm so glad you did!''

"Where are your dominoes?'' Mary asked, glancing at the table which was bare of anything save the
milk and cookies.

"We didn't need them tonight,'' Swinnie said.
"We had other entertainment.''

"Where is Cruise? I'll bet he *was* entertaining.''
Jake looked around the room.

"Asleep. On the sofa.'' Tom pointed into the next
room.

Jake went over to look at his sleeping nephew.
"How did you work that miracle?''

Mary laughed. "Same way they got all seven of us
to go to sleep whenever they baby-sat.'' She sent the
foursome at the table a fond smile.

Jake bundled Cruise into his arms. "Thank you so
much for watching him.''

"Any time,'' Kitty chirped, well pleased with the
looks Mary and Jake were sending each other. Those

two liked each other very well. They'd be eating wedding cake in no time!

"Goodnight," Jake murmured, as he carried Cruise to the front door. "It was nice seeing all of you again."

"Call me next week, Jake," Kitty called out. "I'll show you some properties when you have time in your schedule."

Mary and Jake glanced at each other, this time without the smiles.

Jake nodded briefly. "Thanks, Kitty. I'll call you."

Now that hadn't seemed quite right. Kitty frowned as Mary shut the door behind them. What had been behind that meaningful glance the two had shared?

The foursome waited for Mary to come back in. They could hear the low hum of voices on the porch.

Five minutes later, they were still standing outside talking. Kitty got up nervously to clear the dishes.

"Shall I flicker the porch lights?" Tom asked.

In the girls' teenage years, flickering the porch lights was the signal for whichever van Doorn was saying an overly prolonged goodnight to her beau to come inside before the neighbors started gossiping.

"Heavens, no! Let her stay outside as long as she likes," Kitty snapped. "Mary's no teenager."

At that moment the door opened, and Mary walked inside. Kitty thought she didn't look as happy as she had before. Her heart sinking, she tried to ward off the bad feeling stealing over her.

"Mary?" she asked. "Are you okay?"

"Yes, Kitty. I'm fine." Mary smiled wanly, pale now against the electric-red dress. "Thank you so much for everything you did for me tonight, everyone.''

''Don't thank us, Mary.'' Swinnie came over to give her a hug. ''We were happy to do it.''

''Yep. But it's past our bedtime now.'' Bert hopped up and gave her a fatherly hug. ''Nighty-night, and all that.''

Tom hugged her too, and the two men went out the front door. Like convicts fleeing from a prison, Kitty thought with irritation. ''Is everything all right, Mary? I don't want to be nosy, but of course I am...''

Mary took a deep breath. ''I've talked to Jake about this, Kitty, and he understands.''

''Of course he does, dear. Jake strikes me as one of those rare, empathetic males. What does he understand?''

''That we shouldn't see each other any more,'' Mary explained.

Chapter Seven

"That girl is more stubborn than a mule determined to get into a feed bin!" Kitty sighed as she stared at an unappetizing grilled cheese sandwich in front of her. The foursome sat in the Shotgun Diner trying to eat lunch the day after Mary had set forth her startling news. As much as they liked the cooking, none of them had much room in their stomachs.

Kitty felt like hers was tied in a knot. "I almost think Mary would rather I minded my own business!"

She hadn't known what to say to Mary's pronouncement. Taken by surprise, she had murmured something comforting to Mary about how everything would work out in the end, grabbed Swinnie's hand, and scuttled off into the night after Tom and Bert.

"Well, it's obvious Mary is past the point where we can assist her decision making," Bert intoned. "We'll just have to sit this one out on the sidelines."

Kitty couldn't bear to see the daughters of her best friends move away. It wasn't enough that her best friends, the van Doorn parents, had been stolen from her; did their children have to melt away from her too, like tears from her eyes? "I almost think I've got one of those depression things," she confessed, "and I haven't had one of those fits since my husband died."

"Oh, Kitty." Tom reached over awkwardly and patted her shoulder. "We just can't run these young'uns around anymore. They've gotten older, and so have we."

"It's always hard when your kids decide they'll make their own decisions," Swinnie said with a sigh. "It's so much easier if they'll let us make their decisions for them. With the benefit of our experience and expertise, we could save them so much heartache and pain."

"Mary doesn't want my experience and expertise." Kitty was so sad she was sure she was going to cry. "She wants to make her own mistakes without me helping her."

That didn't come out right, she knew, but her friends were true friends and didn't tease her. They just sat in the booth with her, commiserating quietly.

"I'm no fairy godmother, I know. But we are those girls' only family now. I wouldn't be able to look at myself in the mirror every day if I didn't do my utmost by them." Kitty worked her fingers into a knot. "What sane woman would pass up Jake Maddox? Raven's-wing-black hair, excellent bod, extra-blue eyes, excellent bod, kind and well-mannered—"

"Excellent bod," her friends chorused for her.

"Well, now that you mention it, yes!" Kitty exclaimed. "For heaven's sake, in my day a man like that wouldn't have stayed available for more than two seconds! Matrons with eligible daughters would have swarmed him most eagerly. The only thing Mary swarms is her studying. What did she mean by saying she didn't have time for a relationship right now, anyway?''

There were three shrugs for that particular idiosyncrasy of Mary's.

"Too bad Jake isn't a science," Swinnie said thoughtfully. "Like Jakeology. Jake 101. Quantum Jake Theories. She'd be pulling a 4.0 in those sciences."

"Nah, she'd flunk. Mary only understands those things which relate to humans, not necessarily humans themselves. It's like she knows what makes the heart tick, but not exactly what makes the heart sing and dance around. 'Spect that's a different angle of medicine.'' Bert ran a trembly hand over his shiny head.

"She's adhered to a rigorous schedule so long that she doesn't know how to incorporate any unexpected detours. Her folks' passing was enough.'' Tom shook his head, a little mystified but sympathetic to Mary's ordeal. "I reckon me and Bert's gonna rent a truck to put Mary's and Esther's things in and drive them both out to California.''

"My goodness! I hadn't even thought about that!'' Kitty was dismayed. "They're going to need help getting set up in California.''

"Yep.'' Bert nodded. "We might as well start packing since 'the plan' hasn't gone off too well.''

Kitty's heart felt as if it might slide out of her chest into her white walking shoes. All her spirit was draining out of her. "I don't think I can face it.''

"We're going to have to,'' Bert told her stoically.

"But you might consider having Esther live with you for her senior year."

Kitty perked up. "Esther?" The van Doorn baby live with her, under her auspicious tutelage for an entire year? Her heart sprang to life again, suddenly joyous. There would be the water-tower problem, but she could lock Esther in the basement at night if need be. She could convince the city council not to carry cobalt-blue spray paint in Sunflower Junction for one year. "Of course, Mary's been so immovable lately that one wonders how she would greet the idea of leaving her little sister behind..."

"Probably be a relief. She won't have proper time to spend with her when she's working, and I know she feels guilty about Esther having to graduate from someplace other than home."

"I'll speak to Mary, then!" Kitty exclaimed, her depressed mood instantly evaporating. The "Pop. 22" on the town sign need not be adjusted permanently if Mary didn't move away forever, if she could be enticed into returning one day to Sunflower. It was an idea worth speculating on. "Something good may come of this yet!" she beamed.

MARY DIDN'T FEEL complete relief the way she thought she would after telling Jake she'd simply met him at the wrong time in her life. She liked him far more than she should like any man at this juncture. Jake wasn't just any man, and her prudent heart had spied that right away. She would have recognized that fact even without being manipulated into seeing it. Kitty had told her once, a long time ago when Mary had been struggling through teenage angst, that each person had a soulmate. Once in life, you met your soulmate—if you were very fortunate. By the way things had heated up so quickly between Jake and her, she knew she'd met someone special. The fact that he seemed as smitten with her was heady.

She wondered if she had found her once-in-a-lifetime soulmate—even as she told him goodbye.

That would certainly constitute reckless behavior in a foolhardy sense. Mary did not see herself as foolhardy. She'd been trying so hard to be practical—but what if she'd actually made the mistake of her lifetime? By resisting temptation she'd actually invited misfortune?

Cruise's dislike of her was worrisome, but the nurturing side of her soul wanted to get to know him better. To turn some of those frowns into smiles. To wash away the self-doubt and lack of self-worth she saw in his eyes and replace those feelings with the love every child deserved.

Oh, Jake and his nephew were a tough combination. They'd presented themselves to her, and her heart had cried, "Yes! Yes!"

But her logical mind reminded her that dreams didn't fall into one's lap. They had to be earned, like her medical training, which had to come first and foremost before everything.

Except family, and that took up a healthy chunk of her time and energy. Which was as it should be, but it didn't allow much time for romance.

By the ache in her heart, however, Mary had to admit Kitty had chosen a man who made her want to dream a new dream. A bigger dream. If only she'd been at a different point, if only her parents hadn't passed away, maybe Mary might feel that she was due some reckless behavior.

She was head of the family now, and she owed it to her siblings to set a good example.

Even if it hurt.

JAKE UNDERSTOOD Mary's feelings about not going out with him any more. He didn't like it, but he couldn't disagree with her reasoning. Neither one of them had time for a deep relationship, and neither one of them were the type of people who would enjoy a quick fling. He admired her for her resolve.

He still would like to see her, yet he would respect her wishes and not call on her again. He could certainly understand the overwhelming challenges she was facing.

Consequently, when he picked up the ringing phone and discovered Kitty on the other end, he wondered what she was up to now.

"It's time to find you a home," she sang into his ear.

With Cruise so active, she was more right than she knew. Jake lived in a seventh-floor suite. He was desperately afraid his imp of a nephew would take it into his head to open a window and do some ledge crawling. Still, he knew enough at this point to be suspicious of Kitty's overtures. "Do you have something other than the van Doorn property?" he asked pointedly.

"I just happen to have a newly listed renovated farmhouse that I think will suit you and Cruise fine. Six bedrooms, four with their own baths, the other two could be used for storage or offices. The owners live out of town and don't want to keep it up anymore.''

The faster he and Cruise were settled, the better. He was determined that he and his nephew would spend quality time becoming a family in a place where life stood still in the values Cruise had missed out on.

''There is a fully stocked fish pond on the property,'' Kitty said. ''And a couple acres of wooded property, whether you're of a mind to hunt duck in the fall or merely watch the leaves change colors. Nature is always fascinating to young minds, you know.''

There were certainly no trees around the complex he lived in. An office would be easy enough to set up in a house that size. He had a feeling Kitty was working him like a sheep dog with all of the realtor's finesse she possessed. Yet the farmhouse sounded inviting. ''What time do you want to see us?''

''Two o'clock would be fine.''

He frowned at her business-like, clipped tone, almost as if she was anxious to get off the phone. ''Thanks, Kitty, we'll be there.''

''Good.''

She hung up. He leaned back, dissatisfied. Something had been very different in Kitty's voice, a tautness he hadn't heard before.

MARY RAN TO HER CAR after hanging up the phone. Kitty sounded awful! She had her scared half out of her wits. Her heart was in her throat.

Some doctor I'll make, she chided herself. But

Kitty was at her office working, she'd said, and suddenly began feeling unwell.

Mary edged the pedal a little closer to the floor. She didn't think she could bear it if something was seriously wrong with the woman who was almost a mother to her.

Bursting into the realtor's office, she was astonished to find Jake and Cruise there. "What is going on?" she demanded. Surely Kitty wasn't up to her old tricks!

Cruise was patting Kitty's hand, worry on his little face. Jake was fanning Kitty with a sheaf of papers. He appeared just as worried as Cruise. Kitty sat very still in her wooden chair behind her desk.

"I'm fine, dear," she said, but her voice was tight.

This was no prank to get her to see Jake, Mary realized.

"All of a sudden, she just sat down and said she didn't think she felt very well." Jake's honest blue eyes were wide with concern. "I wanted to take her to a doctor, but she insisted on calling you."

"Oh, Kitty!" Mary hurried to Kitty's side to feel her forehead and monitor her pulse. "Why didn't you let Jake take you to the doctor?"

"You *are* a doctor," Kitty snapped with peeve, quite unlike her normally chirpy self. "Why would I call anyone else? Besides, I'm sure it's just the heat."

It *was* a bit warm in Kitty's office. "Have you been working?"

"Of course! I always work. I had a new property come on the market, and I wanted Jake to see it first. I've been very busy." Her slightly wrinkled face was moist with perspiration. Mary could tell Kitty's blood pressure was elevated, but that could be from fear. She was honestly ill, and Mary desperately wished her friend were in the middle of a match-making stunt instead. She would have been angry, but this horrible feeling of despair inside her was worse. Her gaze caught Jake's. He looked as upset as she.

"Let us take you to a doctor, Kitty," Mary insisted.

"Nonsense. I just want to go home and lie down. Jake, please take me home."

Jake and Mary glanced at each other again. Imperceptibly she moved her head in the negative.

He got her message. Squatting next to Kitty's chair, he said, "Miss Kitty, Mary really prefers that I take you to a hospital, or your physician, if you would rather. But I think we should do as Doctor van Doorn wishes."

Kitty bowed her head with no fight in her. "Mary's a good girl, Jake. I'll let you drive me over to the hospital in Dallas, though I'm sure it will be nothing but a waste of time."

"I'd rather waste time than not have you checked over thoroughly." Mary tried to sound forthright, but her throat had spasms of nervous teary emotion. She patted Kitty's hand before standing. "Why don't I drive you?"

"Because I'm not up to riding in that rattletrap of a truck you've got, and you might as well stay here and keep an eye on Cruise."

It *was* bumpy riding in her pickup, and Kitty would be a lot more comfortable in Jake's nicely air-conditioned car. Still, Mary hated to draw him into their problems, especially after she'd told him she couldn't go out with him any more.

"I don't mind taking her," he said.

His warm baritone was soothing and reassuring. "Thanks, Jake."

"Do you mind watching Cruise for me? It's a lot to ask—"

"No, it's not," she said swiftly. "Esther's at home and can help me. You just get Kitty to the hospital in that nice, *fast* Mercedes of yours."

"I will." As he carefully helped Kitty, he slid his gaze to Mary. She tried to smile but she simply couldn't. Her face muscles felt frozen.

"Be as quick as you can, Jake," she murmured. Kitty had constantly massaged her left shoulder and upper chest area the entire five minutes Mary had been in the office. It would have been pointless to ask Kitty if she hurt anywhere because Kitty would have said no. Kitty thought she was indestructible. But to a doctor's eye, the pain was obvious—and to Mary, alarming.

She swiftly opened the door so Jake could walk Kitty out into the bright sunshine. Her heart sinking, Mary could only hope that Kitty was as indestructible as she thought she was.

Jake helped Kitty into the car before glancing down at Cruise. "Do you mind staying with Miss Mary?"

"Don't like her," Cruise said. But with his eyes on his adored Kitty, his bravado was a bit thin.

"I need to take Miss Kitty to the hospital, and we'll be there for a while. Why don't you go to Mary's house with her, and I'll be back in a few hours?"

Cruise's lip trembled. He glanced back up at Mary, his distaste evident. "Don't want you to go," he said to Jake and Kitty.

"I know." Jake ruffled his nephew's hair. "But I have to make sure Miss Kitty is feeling better, just like I would do for you if you were sick. Okay?"

Realizing he was cornered, Cruise lowered his head. "'Kay."

Jake stood, and Mary's skin tingled as they met each other's gaze. "I'll take good care of him."

"Thanks. I'll take good care of her if she'll let me." Jake got in his car and pulled out of the small parking lot.

Mary's eyes filled with the tears she wouldn't let herself fall victim to in front of Kitty. She sniffled once as she walked back inside the office.

"You cwying?" Cruise asked.

It was probably not a good thing to do in front of a child. Mary shook her head. "No, I'm not." She dabbed at her eyes with her sleeve.

"Cwyin's not good." He ran over and sat in Kitty's chair, picking up her pen to scribble on paper.

"Sometimes it is and sometimes it isn't, I suppose." She wished she could stop, but the tears kept leaking out of the corner of both eyes, like a steady drip of flowing water.

"Mommy says I can't cwy. It gives her a headache."

Mary's tears dried up instantly. What a horrible thing to tell a child! "Um, it won't give me a headache if you cry. Do you want to?"

"Nah." He shook his head, content to doodle.

Mary looked over at the squiggles he drew on the white pad. "That's very nice, Cruise..."

Her voice trailed off as she read the note Kitty had

made to herself. *Talk to Mary about Esther living with me.*

Her lips parted, and the tears started up again. Kitty was doing everything she could to keep the van Doorn family with her in any way, shape or fashion, and Mary hadn't been thinking of what their departure would mean to her. In fact, all she'd been thinking of was her plan, and how she had to stick to it. How to best shepherd her sisters through their parents' deaths. How she could sell the house, and the sunflower business, or the two together, whichever would make a better profit, blah, blah, blah....

But never once had she thought about Kitty, Swinnie, Tom and Bert. She felt very small and selfish. She'd been trying so hard to evade Kitty's obvious plan for her that she'd overlooked her friends.

They had needs, too. And now she might be paying the price for overlooking those needs.

What would I do without her?

Chapter Eight

The immediate problem at hand was Cruise, though Mary was in a full fret about Kitty. She had promised to take care of Cruise, and with his dislike of her, it seemed better to take her mind off of Kitty and meet the challenge before her.

"Would you like to go for a ride in my truck?" she asked him.

"'Kay." He slid down from the chair and headed toward the door.

Mary raised her brows. That had been too easy. "We can stop and get an ice cream cone, if you'd like."

"No."

Not as easy as she'd hoped. "Well, we'll just take a drive for now and you can tell me when you get hungry."

Cruise shrugged, obviously not looking forward to going with Mary. Still, she had a red truck, and those were sometimes fascinating to youngsters. "Do you want to watch TV when we get to my house?"

"No!"

Mary heard the almost desperate emphasis in his

tone. She helped him in the truck and buckled his seatbelt across his lap securely. "Bake cookies?"

"No."

She thought maybe she'd almost had him on that one. It seemed as if he said no on principle, not in the habit of deserting his routine of protest. If there was one thing Mary understood, it was routine. "All right," she said, without offering anything further.

They drove the rest of the way to Sunflower Acres in silence. Once she'd parked the car, Mary got out, walked around to open Cruise's door, and didn't touch his seatbelt. "Can you undo it yourself?"

He unbuckled his seatbelt with awkward child's fingers, then hopped down.

"Excellent," Mary complimented crisply. "Now then, Cruise."

The child glared at her, his feet planted in an aggressive stance.

"I have some work to do in my fields. I'll need your help." She marched over to a large toolshed and began gathering her hat, two pairs of gloves, and a special cutting instrument. When Cruise appeared at her side a moment later, she handed him a large basket. He took it very slowly, his face curious.

"That way." Mary pointed toward her truck. "We'll ride to the field." If he got too tired walking it wouldn't be a problem. The fields were set well back from the house, enough to keep bees and animals from being a problem, but close enough so that the cheerful yellow-orange glow of sunflower petals could be seen from every window on the back of the house.

They climbed into the truck and she drove the short

half-mile to the edge of the field. She noted Cruise's face was lit with interest. Instantly, she knew that the key to Cruise was keeping him busy. They got out and he waited for her instructions.

"Now, you can wear these gloves as a precaution. The sunflowers we're going to pick have kind of bristly stems, rough enough to be uncomfortable. They might be hard on your little hands." She gently helped him put on the child's pair of gloves, left over from a day when she had worn them. They had her name on each glove, and every van Doorn child had owned a pair. A lump rose in her throat. Glorying in their children, her parents had saved many mementoes. But the tending of the sunflowers had been one of the first ongoing lessons she'd learned at her parents' hands, particularly her father's. He spent hours talking to her about the plants, showing her how to cut them just so, teaching her the family trade.

Yet no one had been prouder than he when she'd chosen medicine as her profession. *Smart girl,* he'd said, giving her a hug. *Bright as a sunflower.*

Cruise seemed fascinated by the gloves, delighted to have a grown-up responsibility. Mary smiled. "We use this special clipper, because the stalks of this particular kind of flower are very large." She showed him that the stalk was about the same size or bigger than his wrist. "This tool is very sharp, so I'm going to do the cutting, but you pick out which plant we should harvest first."

He showed her, and she clipped the dinner plate-sized blossom, with a one-foot length of stalk. "Now put this in your basket." She handed him the plant.

"It's heavy!" he cried with astonishment, but manfully, he put his burden into the basket.

"Yes, it is." Mary smiled. She had his full attention. "Let's cut about four of these. I have a project I think you'll like."

AS WORRIED AS JAKE WAS about Kitty, he was equally worried about Mary. Cruise was such a dynamo! Mary was used to order and schedule. His nephew lived by the seat of his pants, always walking that thin edge to see how much disaster he could wreak. Gentle Mary wasn't prepared for such a challenge.

He paced the halls while Kitty was examined. He drank a soda. He tried to read a newspaper. All the while he kept thinking about Mary. He tried calling her several times, but no one answered the phone.

Where is she?

Surely Cruise wasn't on one of his missions of destruction? Even now, she might be running after him through the row of closed shops in the town if he'd taken it into his head not to go with her. He tried again to call her and was swiftly reprimanded by a passing nurse who pointed to the sign that instructed people not to use cell phones in this area of the hospital.

Apologizing, he forced himself to sink into a chair. It had been three hours since Kitty had gone in. Concerned, he imagined the possibility of her suffering a heart attack.

It would be disastrous for Mary, so soon after losing her parents.

He got up and roamed the sitting room again, noticing that his chest felt a bit tight. Maybe he'd join Kitty in a fit of angina.

Surely Cruise is being good. Mary's not used to hellions. I hope she hasn't left any matches lying around.

He tried to call her from a pay phone. Nobody answered. In three hours, Mary hadn't made it home with his nephew.

Something bad had happened, he was certain. Mary was under siege, and he should have warned her. Toilet paper rolls would jam the plumbing and toothpaste would be drying in the carpets. The home that the van Doorns had taken such care with would look like a fallout shelter.

His phone rang in his pocket, startling him. Jerking it out, he answered it, even as he ran outside so as not to upset the medical staff. "Hello?"

"Jake?"

He came to a complete stop. "Steffie?"

"Yeah. It's me."

"Uh, hi." His younger half sister calling him took him completely by surprise. "How are you?"

"Fine." Yet she sounded anything but. "How's Cruise?"

Jake hesitated. "He seems to be adjusting well."

"Oh." She was silent for a few seconds. "That's good."

"How's Mother?" He peered in the hospital window, trying to see if anyone was looking for him. *Please let there be nothing seriously wrong with Kitty.*

"All right, except that she misses Cruise."

Jake's jaw dropped. "Misses...Cruise?" That was

the biggest con he'd heard yet. "Cruise…the handful?"

"Yeah." Steffie didn't sound too convincing.

Jake's heart began a slow, uncomfortably heavy beat in his chest. The silence strained, but he couldn't speak. Their mother had never missed anyone. Her complete focus was on herself.

"I kind of miss him, too."

If he didn't know better, he'd think she was reading from a script. Her voice held no emotion, just rote words. He scratched the back of his neck and glanced back inside to look for Kitty. "Look, Steffie, I'm kind of busy right now. Cruise is fine, there's nothing to worry about."

She didn't reply.

"Is there something else you want to talk about? Because I really need to get running."

"No, I just want you to know that I miss him."

His patience wore out. "What are you saying, Steffie? That you want him back?"

"No!" she exclaimed, definitely off the script now. "I just want you to remember that I cared about my kid!"

The phone went dead. Jake automatically turned to see if he could pick up the signal from another direction, but there was no sound. Steffie had definitely hung up on him.

"Great," he muttered. "Just what I need. More confusion."

He wondered briefly why he couldn't have been born into a family with normally functioning brains and hearts. They were bizarrely shaped puzzle pieces which refused to fit together.

Not like the people he'd met in Sunflower Junction. Mary and her family, Kitty and crew, they all had their problems, but they all cared about each other too. At least when Kitty manipulated she did it for a good cause. The cause of Steffie's fake concern and melodramatic phone call would only be revealed when she chose to reveal it.

Striding back inside, he was relieved when a nurse came over to get him. "You can take Kitty May home now."

"She's all right?" His chest instantly lost its tightness.

"Oh, yes." The elderly nurse smiled at his concern. "She's quite a character."

He smiled. "What was bothering her?"

"I'll let her tell you," the nurse said with a secretive smile. Her eyes twinkled behind her glasses. "I see you're everything she claimed you'd be, though."

With that cryptic remark, the nurse steered him toward Kitty's room. She sat up on a gurney, nothing escaping her bright eyes.

"Are you feeling better, Kitty?"

"I am, and ready to be released from this jail." She sprang down before he could assist her. "Take me home, Jake. I've got a lot to do today, much too much to be bothered by those pearl onions I ate for lunch. Actually, they were closer to the size of ping pong balls rather than pearls, but they sure were good, and I do so love my onions."

Jake grimaced in sympathy. He'd stay away from pearl onions if Kitty ever offered him any. Grinning, he helped her into the hallway.

"Reckon your little dickens of a nephew is giving

Mary a run for her money. We'd best go check on them.''

"Shouldn't you go home and rest?" Jake glanced back toward a nurse, intending to ask if there were any instructions Kitty should be following.

"Nope. I'm fit as a fiddle!" She looked well-satisfied with herself. "I just worry too much about Mary, you know."

He paused at the doleful note in her voice. "Mary seems like she's doing fine, considering everything she's tackling."

"Oh, I know." Her voice wavered a bit, and her eyes softened tremulously. "She's a brave girl, throwing herself on a pyre of sacrifice for her family."

Kitty took baby steps toward the parking lot. He grasped her arm gently, assisting her. "Miss Kitty, I know what you're doing, and it can't work. Mary has made up her mind where I'm concerned, and I'm content to do as she wishes."

"Are you?" Kitty honored him with a raised eyebrow.

"Yes, I am," he said firmly. "Frankly, I wish I'd had as much determination concerning my studies as she does."

"You've done fine for yourself. And your lack of degree matters not one whit to Mary, so that is a pathetically thin excuse."

"Yes, but I could have done better with my education. I understand what it means to her. I admire Mary for continuing even in the face of opposition."

She snorted. "You mean me. You think I'm a pest."

He laughed out loud. "I mean her circumstances,

and yes, possibly your matchmaking at times. But I deeply appreciate your efforts, Kitty. You've changed my life for the better by introducing me to her.''

"Have I?''

"Yes.'' This was an indisputable fact. "I know exactly what I want for Cruise now that I've seen it at Sunflower Acres.''

"Hard to emulate loving relationships if you haven't experienced it yourself,'' she said shrewdly. "You'll need help. My Mary could give you that assistance.''

Fortunately, the car wasn't but two more steps away. He was going to pack Miss Kitty into a seat and turn on the radio so she couldn't issue any more pronouncements like that one.

"I see the seeds of great potential in you, Jake,'' Kitty said softly, her hand on his forearm slightly pressuring him into halting and staring down into her eyes. "I think you'll make another mistake you'll always regret, like giving up your education, if you give up on Mary.''

"LOOK, UNCLE JAKE, LOOK!'' Cruise yelled with delight when he saw his uncle getting out of the car with Kitty. "Look what I made!''

Instead of disaster, which had kept his stomach in a knot the entire drive back from Dallas, Jake found his nephew dirty, happy and proud of himself.

Mary helped Kitty from the car, sweeping her into a gentle embrace. "You had me so worried!''

She turned to face Jake, pink-flushed from heat and wearing one smudge of dirt across her nose—and eminently more desirable because of it. They smiled at each other, and Jake felt a spreading trail of desire creep into him, a deep warmth soothing away the knot of tension balled in his stomach. "Everything went fine?"

"Yes." She wouldn't release Kitty, but she smiled at Cruise. "We did just fine."

Cruise couldn't wait another moment. He grabbed Jake by the hand and pulled him over to one of the many live oak trees shading the front and side lawns of the house. "Look!" He pointed to a large, fat sunflower which had been securely tied against the tree trunk. "We made birdfeeders!"

"Natural birdfeeders." Mary came to stand beside them. "Cruise chose his sunflowers, then we brought them back here and tied them to the trees. He stood on a ladder, of course, to assist me."

Cruise's face shone with pride at his accomplishment. "The squirrels are going to eat the seeds!"

Mary laughed. "Mostly squirrels. Occasionally a bird gets a bite, but usually the squirrels hog most the most. The mourning doves like what gets dropped on the ground, though."

"The seeds are inside." Cruise squirmed for Jake to lift him up, which he did. "See that?"

He pointed with one small finger, and Jake peered inside the wide face of the sunflower. Radial rows of orderly, black-striped white seeds packed tightly together inside. "I didn't know that was how sunflower seeds were grown."

"Yes. It's a fun crop for kids." Mary smiled at Jake, and a glow of happiness seemed to light her face. Jake thought she had never looked more beautiful than in the dirt, gardening gloves, sun hat and cap-sleeved, calf-length blue dress she wore. Her aquamarine eyes sparkled, and her cheeks were kissed with a glow from being outdoors. A little trail of perspiration dotted a trail between her breasts, and Jake swallowed hard.

"We'd better get Miss Kitty inside so she can sit down," he said, trying not to think about kissing Mary.

"Absolutely not!" Kitty said with asperity. "I'm going home since you've got the scamp eating out of the palm of your hand. I've caused enough trouble today."

"You're going inside to have a glass of iced tea and a rest in the air conditioning. I want to hear all about your trip to the hospital." Mary took Cruise by the hand and walked toward the porch. "We'll wash you up and then you can set out the cookies, since you're such a good helper," she told him.

"Well, it's not a trip to the State Fair, I can tell you." Kitty bristled. "So that's all you need to know," she called after Mary. "Jake, if you'll run me back to my office, I'll drive myself home."

"I think Mary's got a good idea. You should take her up on her offer."

"If anything, I should be showing you that renovated farmhouse." Kitty jutted her lip at him. "Me staying under your feet isn't going to help you change Mary's mind about seeing you," she said in a low tone which didn't lack purpose.

He laughed and took the matchmaker by the arm, leading her toward the house. "I have no intention of trying to change her mind. I happen to think she's right about her goal."

"You'll regret letting her go," Kitty warned.

"I know. I'd regret stopping her even more." He gave her a solemn look. "Not that I don't appreciate your advice on the matter. But Mary would be unhappy if she wasn't following her heart."

Kitty stopped to stare up at him as they reached the porch. "You're falling in love with her, aren't you?"

He gave her a wry smile. "Maybe just a little. Satisfied?"

She cocked her head at him. "Somehow, no. There's nothing satisfying about unrequited love."

"How about you and I keep it our little secret then?" He helped her up the steps. "You need some iced tea and air conditioning, and I'll just be content to be around Mary. All right?"

"Faint heart never won fair maiden," Kitty sighed under her breath. "Mr. May clean swept me off my feet before I had a chance to think about the consequences. And I was happy every minute we had together!"

"Kitty, I heard every word of that." Mary opened the door, her expression a bit stern. "At least the last part, anyway. Would you please quit encouraging Jake to sweep me off my feet?"

Mary's eyes met his with some embarrassment. He hoped the last part was *all* she'd heard. Nothing like Mary knowing he was falling for her to make her avoid him like a bee sting. "I keep telling her you can't be swept," he said mildly, helping Kitty past Mary into the refreshingly cool indoors. "And I'm not much good with a broom, anyway."

"Well, that's one strike against you then," Mary said with some humor.

"Do you want to be swept?" He raised his eyebrows at her.

"Certainly not!"

Kitty sighed. "You can't ask a woman if she wants to be swept. That's not sweeping, Jake. No woman's going to admit that she wants a man to just—" she made a sweeping motion with her hand "—romance her until she says yes when all along she's been digging in her heels!" She gazed up at him over Mary's shoulder. "The independent ones always dig in their heels."

"Cookies!" Cruise hollered from the kitchen.

Mary sent an exasperated look Jake's way before hurrying to help Cruise with the chore he'd been assigned. That look said *Don't you dare listen to a word out of her mouth!*

He shook his head as Kitty sat down. Contrary to what Miss Kitty believed, Mary was not a good candidate for being "swept." He wouldn't be able to handle that job, anyway. His family had taught him one thing: Nothing went smoothly in a home where people resented everything about each other.

Mary had said this was the wrong time in her life to get serious about someone. He intended to honor her feelings.

Just like Cruise, he needed to be wanted and loved.

Not that he didn't wish Mary felt the same way he did.

"I want to stay here forever, Uncle Jake." His nephew gazed up at him with hero adoration. "I like it here."

Mary and Kitty halted in their passing out of tea and cookies from the tray.

Jake tried to act as if he hadn't thought the very same thing. "It is a nice place, Cruise."

"Can we stay?" His face turned up to Jake with his eyes full of pleading.

Kitty glanced at Mary as if to say, *See? Even Cruise agrees that you all three belong together!*

Mary met Jake's eyes slowly. "It's not such a bad idea, Jake. I know you're looking for a place to buy. You mentioned this property was too big, but I could sell the house separately and sell the sunflower business to someone else. Of course, with your business expertise, you could probably make the business side flourish."

Her gaze was admiring of his corporate acumen, but his heart pounded as her meaning sunk in. She really was going to sell her home, and none of Kitty's machinations could change her mind. Again, he understood her motivation. How could she hang on to a place where she had no intention of living?

"I'd rather you two live here than strangers. And I've talked to Esther, Kitty. She'd be delighted to stay with you." She smiled a little shamefacedly. "I saw the notepad at your office."

Kitty gaped, not sure if she was pleased or upset.

"Can we, Uncle Jake? Can we?" Cruise demanded, his eyes shining.

Jake glanced at the three of them as he considered her proposition. Mary would get what she wanted: freedom to leave. He supposed Kitty would get something she wanted: companionship. Cruise and he would get what they wanted: a wonderful home where they could build on their relationship. And yet, Jake had the strangest feeling that none of them would be getting exactly what they *needed*.

Or even wanted most. Somehow, it was all tied up in Mary, and he of all people understood why she couldn't continue to be part of their lives.

Chapter Nine

What made Mary suddenly offer to sell her house to Jake she didn't know. She was upset about Kitty's sudden chest pains, despite the onion excuse. Perhaps Esther staying with Kitty would give Mary peace of mind that Kitty wasn't alone. Esther deserved the stability of graduating from the place where she'd grown up among her friends. Certainly Jake and Cruise were perfect buyers for her house.

Mary was at her wits' end trying to figure everything out. It seemed better to get rid of one of the major stresses in her life so that she could focus, and what to do with the property was definitely stressing her.

But Jake was a bigger stressor. She'd nearly died of mortification when she'd heard Kitty encouraging him to romance her. Of all things she did not want, it was Jake Maddox feeling like he had to date her. She was very cognizant that Kitty had been the push *and* the shove behind Jake's pursuit of her.

What man would want a scholarly old maid like her?

Kitty looked very expectant at this turn of events.

It was clear she had decided Mary's offer was auspicious—for what reason, Mary wasn't sure.

"Why don't we discuss your offer later?" Jake asked easily. "It's certainly something to think about."

Kitty smiled, and kept her thoughts to herself for once—and that made Mary acutely uneasy. Had she unwittingly fallen prey to one of Kitty's schemes? She glanced at Jake, suspicious, but he just shrugged as if he knew what she was thinking but didn't have the answer. Cruise and Kitty went off to watch TV, leaving her sitting at the table with Jake.

"Are you in cahoots with her?" Mary demanded.

"I don't think so. I'm not sure she'd let me in on it if I were." He grinned. "I've got a lot of experience in the business world, but Kitty moves on a completely different level. Her motives aren't for profit, so I haven't seen her brand of horse-trading before."

Mary rolled her eyes. "That isn't exactly comforting." Pursing her lips, she watched Jake bite into another cookie. Every move he made was done with grace and good manners. She wished she didn't feel so awkward. "I appreciate you taking her to the hospital. I was so nervous I don't know that I could have driven."

"Doctor van Doorn nervous?"

He grinned and reached over to pat her hand, which did nothing to soothe her unsettled feeling.

"Yes." She glanced at him shyly. "Kitty is a mess, but I love her."

He leaned close. "I'll bet I was more nervous than you were."

"Really? Was she in a lot of pain?" Mary couldn't bear to think of Kitty suffering.

"She didn't seem to be too bad, just uncomfortable." He traced small circles across her hand which made the moment between them seem very intimate. "I couldn't stop thinking about what torture Cruise was visiting on you. I called several times, and when I didn't get an answer, I feared the worst."

She laughed. "What could one little boy do, Jake? He was a perfect angel the entire time."

He frowned at her. "You slipped him something. Or cast him under a spell."

"No, really. I'll admit, knowing that he didn't like me at first was worrisome, but he seemed anxious to participate in our project."

Jake nodded, and pulled her hand into his, cupping it with his other. "I'm really getting a good feeling about Cruise, although I've only had him a few days. I think there's a good kid inside him who just wants to be loved."

"Isn't that what everyone wants?" Mary asked.

Her question hung between them as they stared into each other's eyes.

"At some level, of course," she said hurriedly. Talk about enchantments! She was falling under Jake's!

"Of course," he murmured.

He held her hand up to his lips, gently caressing it. Butterfly tickles ran all over her skin. Her gaze stayed locked with his, her breath caught dizzily in her chest.

The sound of loud snoring broke the spell. Mary jerked her hand away from Jake and jumped to her feet. Quietly, crossing into the den, she saw that both

Cruise and Kitty were asleep. He was in her lap, his head resting against her shoulder, and Kitty's head had fallen back against the sofa so that she snored.

"I'd better take him home," Jake said from behind her, making her start.

"I should take Miss Kitty home, too. She can't be comfortable like that." But even as she said it, she turned to Jake, her eyes full of question. He slid his hands along her arms and then to her waist, pulling her toward him. She tipped her head back, wanting him to kiss her. Without hesitating, Jake accepted the invitation. Closing her eyes, Mary allowed herself to fall into the sensation of Jake's desire for her.

She wished it didn't ever have to end.

"HEARD YOU MADE A RUN to the quack shack yesterday," Bert commented to Kitty as the foursome seated themselves at the barrel the next afternoon.

"And full of quacks it was, too," Kitty asserted disparagingly. "Mary could have told me the same thing they told me and saved me a bundle. She's the only doctor worth a flip, to my mind. And one of those unfortunate babies fresh out of nursing school hooked the heart monitor up to me backwards." She shook her head in disgust. "All to tell me I'd eaten too many onions, and that I was fretting too much. When I worry, I tighten up my chest muscles over my heart, apparently. That's the kind of doctorin' you get from young kids who never ate a pearl onion in their lives."

"Just don't know about young folks these days," Tom murmured. "Seems that they're lacking something."

"Good upbringing," Swinnie said decisively. "That's what they lack."

"And Mary's got that in abundance." Kitty leaned close to take them into her confidence, though there was no one else in the bait shop. "But she lacks something crucial, and that's the female instinct."

"How so?" Bert asked, opening a root beer.

"Well, Jake is in love with her."

"He is?" Swinnie clapped her hands. "What wonderful news!"

Kitty waved that off. "Yes, except Mary would never acknowledge that he might be in love with her. And she plain will not be strayed from her plan." She leaned back, giving them all a wise look. "If you could have heard the smooching going on behind the sofa last night, you'd have bet double or nothing that there'd be a wedding right along with Eve's."

"No!" Swinnie breathed. "Were they really smooching?"

"Sounded like Cupid just wouldn't quit on 'em. They oughta have chapped lips this morning!" she said with glee.

"How come they were kissing behind the sofa?" Tom wanted to know.

"Yeah, how come you could hear all this lip-locking?" Bert inquired.

"They thought I was asleep. And I might have gone out for a second, until the sound of valentine firecrackers awakened me. I had to pretend I was still asleep for a solid ten minutes!" Kitty giggled to herself, remembering. "I don't believe even Mr. May ever kissed me for a full ten minutes."

"Probably 'cause you never shut up long enough

for him to stick to your face." Bert shook his head. "I haven't heard any reason to put up my money double or nothing that there's going to be a wedding."

"That's because we have to up the ante. As her stand-in parents, godparents that we are, I put forth that it's up to us to see to Mary's well-being in this matter." Kitty gave up pretending to look at her dominoes. "Mary thinks she's going to sell Jake her house. I say that's all fine and good, but it isn't a plan unless Jake and Mary are living under the same roof." She gave them an eagle-eyed stare. "Jake has been extremely reluctant to encourage Mary to think upon him as a serious candidate for a walk down ye old aisle."

"So you're saying he needs an incentive," Swinnie guessed.

Kitty nodded. "Exactly. And it's gotta be a good one, because lady and gents, Mary's been packing her boxes. In the old days, a dowry would have been proffered. Today's times call for a more direct business approach."

The foursome gazed down at the barrel, lost in their own thoughts. The fish freezer wheezed in the corner, but that was the only sound in the black-and-white-linoleum-floored room.

"I know!" Bert snapped his fingers. "We'll offer Jake a year's worth of free bait if he'll marry our girl!"

"Does he even like to fish?" Tom asked.

"Everyone likes to fish. What normal man doesn't?" Bert shot back in disgust.

"No, no, no." Kitty shook her head impatiently.

"I don't think you two understand the gravity of the situation. A year's worth of live worms and minnows is not an enticing dowry."

"A longhorn?" Swinnie suggested.

"What would he do with a longhorn?" Kitty demanded, her eyes fairly bugging with astonishment at that ridiculous idea.

"I don't know!" Swinnie wailed. "It's better than cups full of icky squirming earthworms, though!"

"That's debatable," Bert grumbled. "I'd rather have the bait."

"De-*bait*-able?" Tom smirked. "Get it?" When everyone favored him with a dour expression, he shrugged and continued fiddling with his latest electrical toy. "We could get up a collection to send Esther off to a fancy girls' summer camp for the next two weeks so that Mary and Jake can have the house to themselves."

"No!" Kitty exclaimed. "That's cruel, Tom! Besides, there's Cruise, and he's more of an impediment than poor Esther, my baby."

"Okay, so we ship Cruise off to boot camp for tots, and—"

"Absolutely not," Kitty overruled. "That tyke is coming along nicely under my influence." She scrunched her face in a knot of concentration. "It has to be huge, it has to be stupendous, something Jake can't get anywhere else, not even in Dallas…"

They all stared at her for inspiration.

She fairly glowed with the sudden burst of brainstorm. "If Jake gets Mary to marry him and they live at Sunflower Acres, we…will…" she made certain she had their undivided, breathless attention, "*Name the town after him!* Maddox, Texas!'' she cried with delighted enthusiasm at having the biggest idea at the barrel.

Three faces stared back at her blankly.

"Maddox, Texas, sounds stupid," Bert announced.

"No more stupid than 'Pop. 13' is going to look on our town sign!" Kitty snapped, annoyed by his lack of awe. "How in heck are we ever going to rebuild our town if it's a pin-dot on the map, a ghost town of deserted buildings?" She jutted her chin stubbornly.

"She has a point," Tom said slowly. "I could live with Maddox, Texas." He put the electric whatsit on the table so he could concentrate on Kitty's light bulb of an idea.

"I could, too, if it means we get to reopen Sunflower Junction Elementary. Or would it be Maddox Elementary, then?" Swinnie blinked as she thought this through.

"Let's not put the cart before the horse." Kitty was well-satisfied with the kernel of her idea. "Bert, as mayor of this town, you're elected to do your civic duty and present our offer to Jake."

"Me?" Bert nearly knocked the barrel over as he recoiled. "I ain't putting forth such a hare-brained scheme—" He paused as three people stared back at him grimly. "Don't you think the fish-bait idea had more general appeal?" After receiving no reply, he said, "Couldn't we go as a committee?"

They shook their heads at him.

"You're the honorable spokesperson for the town." Tom slapped him on the back. "Let's go eat at the Shotgun. I'm about to starve to death after all this plotting.''

"I'd rather starve to death than make such a fool of myself," Bert griped. "I submit that we ought to be minding our own beeswax. Look what trouble we got ourselves into with the Wife Raffle and the easy rider!''

Kitty smiled to herself as the foursome headed to the door. There was no cause for worry. A businessman like Jake couldn't fail to be tempted by the wonderful offer he would shortly receive.

JAKE HAD THOUGHT THROUGH Mary's offer all night after he and Cruise returned to his seventh-floor condo. His home was so sterile, so gray and cold after the warmth of Sunflower Acres.

Today he and Cruise sat across from Mary in the Shotgun Diner, ready to make an offer on the house. He couldn't keep his mind on business, though. The fact was, Mary did a lot to warm him up. He felt drawn to her, he drank her in, like crops did sunshine. When he was around Mary, he felt certain that the winter he'd known in his life might be gone for good.

His dilemma was actually simple. She was going to leave, and it was only a matter of time before she found another buyer. Since Cruise liked being at Sunflower Acres so much, he should probably stop focusing on the fact that Mary wouldn't be there and just draw up a contract. That would make two happy people, Cruise and Mary.

Sitting across the table from her, he wondered why it was so hard to negotiate for her house. He would have paid the moon to have *her*. Knowing how important it was to her to be able to move toward putting in her final time toward her medical training, he swallowed back his feelings.

"This is harder than I thought it would be," she said, an uncertain smile on her face. "I know I'm doing the right thing. I'm lucky to be able to sell to someone who wants the whole thing, lock, stock and barrel." Mary sighed, sparkly tears starting to fill her eyes. "It's not a matter of money. I can't see the practicality of hanging on to a home where none of us will live, yet I think it's going to break my heart to say goodbye to the place my family lived."

He hardly knew what to say to that. Somehow, he felt like the Big Bad Wolf when he meant to be a Knight in Shining Armor. Maybe it was best to change the subject for a while—Mary appeared to be on the brink of tears and he couldn't bear to see her cry. "So. I've never asked what kind of doctor you're going to be."

"Oh," she said, all sniffly. "A pediatrician."

"A pediatrician. Now that fully explains why you don't see a reason to stay in Sunflower. No children to make well."

She smiled a bit. "Well, there'd be Cruise. Aren't you going to mind him not having playmates?"

He was glad to see the smile light her face. "Not right away. He and I need to get to know each other. Maybe by the time he's school-age Kitty will have snared some van-driving families to move out here."

"What made you come out to Sunflower Junction anyway? It's not exactly a thriving bedroom community."

He shrugged. "I wanted a peaceful area. Land

where Cruise can run and play.'' Ruffling the little boy's hair, he said, ''I'd like to have grown up in a smaller town myself.''

''So it's your dream.''

''Yeah. Everybody wants something different from what they've had, I guess.'' He'd had uncaring people in his life; he was certainly drawn to Mary, who cared about everybody. Reaching across the table, he smoothed a gentle palm along her cheek. ''You move to the city, I'll move to the country.''

The solution didn't seem quite that satisfactory.

''Jake, listen.'' She glanced at him shyly. ''I...I thought this was a good idea. In my heart I know I have to do this. It's just that...it's harder than I thought it would be.'' Her eyes pleaded with him.

''No problem.'' He patted her hand where it lay clutching a fork, though she hadn't eaten a bite. ''We'll talk about it when you're ready.''

''I don't know why I'm...acting this way—'' She sniffled again. ''Oh, for heaven's sake. Here come Kitty and crew. If Kitty sees me weepy, she'll get to fixing whatever she thinks is wrong with me. I'm going to go wash my face.''

''I'll hold them at bay.''

She jumped up and hurried to the ladies' room. Jake shook some more ketchup on Cruise's fries and braced for the invasion of the wonderful, well-meaning matchmakers. If they could figure out a way for him to end up with Mary, they'd be miracle workers indeed.

To his astonishment, they only waved as they seated themselves at the front of the restaurant. Jake saluted in return, then went back to eating, very surprised by the fact that he hadn't been descended upon.

After a moment, Bert appeared at Jake's table, hat in hand.

Uh-oh, too much to hope for. Cruise glanced up as he dragged another fry through the ketchup in his plastic, paper-lined basket.

"Howdy, Jake," Bert said hesitantly.

"Hiya, Bert." Jake nodded, noticing that the older man seemed distinctly uncomfortable, if the accordion he was twisting his hat into was any indication. "How are you?"

"Oh, fine, fine." Bert nodded. "Just fine."

"Glad to hear it," Jake said wryly. "Going to get a bite to eat?"

"Yes, I think we will. The steak fingers are good. And the mashed potatoes are home-made," he continued, listing the menu as if Jake wasn't already eating.

"I'll try those next time."

"Good, good. You know, this is the only restaurant in Sunflower Junction," Bert mentioned. "Once there was another little joint but the health inspector threatened to close it down so the guy went ahead and closed up shop. And we've got an old fellow who cooks burgers on a grill in his yard on Friday nights, but that's about all the eats you get around here." He shrugged. "'Course, if we had more people move here we might have a chance at a better selection of grub. You know?"

"I understand completely. Could happen," Jake said non-committally. He had a feeling the foursome wanted to know if he was purchasing Mary's house.

Right now, he wasn't going to give them anything on which to speculate. Mary had been too upset, and he wasn't going to discuss it if she wasn't ready.

Bert shifted from foot to foot. "Well, I'll let you get back to your chow." He backed away from the Formica-topped table. "Good talking to ya."

"You, too." Jake casually waved at the three craning occupants of the table as Bert shuffled back that way. "He was up to something, Cruise." He glanced over his shoulder in time to see Kitty, Tom and Swinnie rain crumpled paper napkins on Bert. "They're *all* up to something."

Mary's head poked around the edge of the restroom door. She instantly pulled back and closed it again. Jake wondered at her sudden retreat until Bert reappeared at his elbow.

"Uh, Jake?"

"Yes, Bert?"

He stuffed his hat onto his head and hooked his thumbs in his jeans. "As the Honorable Mayor of Sunflower Junction, I'd like you to know that we'd welcome you with open arms should you consider moving to this town, although it has no grocery store. We'd consider you and Cruise an asset, and would do everything we could to make y'all part of the community. In other words, you'd be amongst friends."

Jake was moved. "Thanks, Bert. It's good to know."

Bert's Adam's apple moved rapidly up and down in his throat as he struggled for his next words. "As the Honorable Mayor of Sunflower Junction, I'd like to lay a proposition on the table for your due consideration."

No doubt they wanted him to open a business of some kind which might bring some prosperity to the dried-up town. "What's on your mind?"

"I noticed you seem to be keen on Mary." He hesitated. "You know she's a highly eligible young lady. Unattached, too, if you know what I mean."

He *did* know—Kitty had made sure he knew only about a hundred times. But he wouldn't embarrass any of the foursome by revealing that their efforts were about as subtle as a building on fire.

"I'm glad I met her. She's a great lady." Jake swallowed and wished Bert would get to his point.

"Yes, yes, that she is." Bert rocked back on his heels. "Jake, here's the situation. If you could see your way clear to wedding our sweet gal and settling down in Sunflower Junction, we're prepared to put a proposition before the city council—that's mostly me and Tom and Swinnie and Kitty—that the town name be changed to reflect your mighty welcome presence. We propose to change our humble little place on the map to Maddox, Texas, home of Jake Maddox, a growing mecca where big dreams turn into bigger dreams!" he finished with a flourish and a proud grin. "Just say the word, Jake, and we'll order the sign!"

Chapter Ten

Jake hardly knew what to reply to Bert's outrageous proposal. The older man was totally serious. His knuckles were clenched and white on his hat as he stared at Jake.

Holding back his disbelief, Jake made certain it didn't show on his face. He didn't want to hurt Bert's feelings, but out of respect for Mary, it was time to make Kitty and crew understand that what they wanted couldn't be manipulated.

"Bert, listen," he said gently. "Don't you think Mary ought to have a say in her future?"

"Well, of course," Bert said huffily. "It's just that maybe she's not thinking clearly right now. Grief and all that."

A small smile tugged at Jake's lips. "I appreciate your proposal. I'm flattered that you think so much of me. But the fact is, Mary's got a dream. And she's going to leave, Bert," he said, keeping his voice very soft so the words wouldn't be too harsh. "I know it's hard on all of you."

He glanced toward the front table. Three gray-topped heads whipped in opposite directions, as if they hadn't been straining to read his every facial expression. "I know you don't want Mary to leave. Part of me wishes she wouldn't, too. But she has to do something for Mary, don't you think?"

"What do you mean?" Bert demanded.

Jake rubbed his chin. "It seems to me that she's got her sisters keeping her busy. She's trying to plan a wedding for Eve and worrying about Esther's education. The twins are a load on her mind right now. Rachel rode off, and Mary's not certain that was a good idea. She's helping Joan get ready for her summer mini-courses she's taking in Dallas so she can get a few credits out of the way. What does that leave for Mary?"

Bert was silent.

"I've got my own bundle of energy, which would only add to her to-do list," he said with a glance at Cruise. Not to mention that Kitty and crew added their own demands on her time. "The last thing I want to be is one more person taking from Mary. If anything, I want to give her something she wants."

Bert looked hopeful. "I'm *sure* she'd love a *big* wedding ring!"

Jake laughed. "I'm not as convinced of that as you are." He could tell Bert was paying no attention to his reasoning. Best to let the old guy go with some dignity. His friends were going to give him a hard enough time as it was for failing on his mission. "I'll keep your proposition in mind," he said, with a very serious expression.

"Oh, good!" Bert breathed. "I'm mighty pleased to hear that."

"I don't know that I'd be accepted by the lady in

question." Jake wondered if that was the way to solve this matter. He could tell Kitty and the gang that Mary had turned him down. She would, so it wouldn't be exactly like he was fibbing.

An uncomfortable thought hit him. Maybe he was flattering himself just a bit *too* much. What if they decided to hunt up another man for Mary if they thought Jake wasn't up to the challenge?

It was a terrible thought. Here he was trying not to step on Mary's dream—and he just might find himself being replaced by some guy who lacked his principles.

"Thank heavens they're gone!" Mary slid into the seat facing him.

He glanced over his shoulder. To his astonishment, they'd made a fast exit. He'd figured they'd hang around to see if he'd duly execute their proposition.

"What did they want?" She looked at him, curiosity alive in her warm, intelligent eyes, and Jake felt a sudden kick of jealousy that he might be dumped in favor of a less fair-minded knight.

Yet he couldn't tell Mary about The Proposition. She'd have a fit.

"You marry Uncle Jake?" Cruise asked in a little-boy voice, his eyebrows soaring upward under his dark locks of tousled hair.

Mary stared at the child. "What?"

Jake snatched the ketchup bottle and began shaking it vigorously into Cruise's basket. "Do you want anything else to eat, Cruise?"

"No." Cruise pushed the basket away.

Mary looked at Jake. "Did he say what I think he just said?"

"Well, maybe." He gave her a smile that felt very weak. "I mean, I'm not sure what you think he just said. Anything is possible."

"I thought…" she hesitated, frowning. "I thought he wanted to know if I was going to marry you."

"Oh!" Jake drummed his fingers against the Formica. "*That's* what you thought he said."

Mary waited, her aquamarine eyes large and questioning. Her blond brows sat in tiny furrows of curiosity. He shrugged. "I didn't hear what he said exactly. Not *precisely.*"

"*I said,*" Cruise repeated in an extremely loud, petulant, soprano child's voice, "you marry Uncle Jake?"

Diners at a nearby booth turned to stare. Jake shrugged sheepishly. "See? That's what you thought he said. You were right."

Mary appeared worried. Jake thought that was a bad sign.

"Maybe he means M-a-r-y, as in Mary and Uncle Jake," he offered. "Not like m-a-r-r-y Uncle Jake."

She held his gaze, obviously not convinced. "Have you been discussing something with Cruise that I should know about?"

"I…don't think so."

Mary's eyelashes lowered, and Jake thought hard. "I mean, he could have thought about it on his own. Marrying, er, Mary, I mean."

"Little people don't usually, do they, unless they've heard it from an adult?"

"I couldn't say, myself. Parenting is new to me." He shook his head with a silly grin and decided to change the subject. "I guess—"

"I can't answer your question, Cruise," Mary said kindly. "I'm not sure what you want to know."

Cruise drew himself up to deliver another proclamation. "Don't want you marry Uncle Jake!"

Heads turned again. Mary blushed, and Jake wasn't so sure he didn't feel his neck flushing, too.

"I think I now get the context of your original question, Cruise." Mary's gaze skipped to Jake. "What do you have to say for yourself?"

Jake gulped and jumped headlong into the fire. "There may have been some discussion of you marrying me," he hedged, hoping Cruise would keep further revelations to himself.

"Oh, Jake," Mary said on a sigh. "That's so sweet. No one has ever wanted to marry me."

"Yeah, well. You've dated a bunch of idiots, then," he mumbled.

Her eyes were shining. Jake felt like his mouth was glued shut. Was she waiting for a proposal? Had she already accepted? Were they on their way—to what? Her living in California and him living in Sunflower? He hung helplessly, waiting for her to speak.

She didn't say a word.

Apparently he was supposed to elaborate.

"Bert says you are," Cruise accused.

Mary frowned. "Bert? How does he know?"

Jake spread his palms open in a *What-can-you-expect-from-the-mouth-of-babes?* gesture.

"Wait a minute! He talked to you while I was in the ladies' room, didn't he?" she demanded.

"He came over to say hi," Jake admitted.

"He must have said a lot more if Cruise is asking if I'm marrying you and you look like you're in a place you wish you weren't!'' Mary glared at him. ''Did Bert ask you to ask me to marry you?''

''Well—'' Jake began.

''Yes!'' Cruise asserted, glaring at Mary. ''Uncle Jake is going to marry me!''

Both adults digested that for a moment.

''Uh, I can't marry you, Cruise,'' Jake said.

''Why not?''

''Because I can only marry a woman. A mommy. Daddies marry mommies,'' he explained.

''Don't care. I'm still going to marry you when I grow up.'' He sent Mary his most belligerent look.

''I think that's a fine idea, Cruise,'' Mary said gently, yet managing to send Jake a close-your-mouth! warning with her eyes. ''You should do that. And I don't want to marry your uncle anyway.''

''You don't?'' Jake demanded. There for a moment, she'd seemed kind of happily weepy-eyed. Like maybe he might be getting a yes he hadn't been expecting today. Not that he knew how the heck they'd work out the bumps, but he'd sure been willing to discuss it.

That's when the truth hit him.

He hadn't even blinked about the notion of proposing to her, of saying ''Two tickets, please,'' to the merry-go-round of marriage. Hadn't heard one word from the voice that had repeatedly reminded him over the years that marriage wasn't for him if he had to suffer the way his parents had suffered from their lack of respect for each other and their marriage.

In fact, he felt suddenly, surprisingly hurt by her avowal that she wouldn't marry him.

The tight knot in his stomach was testimony to one

overriding fact. Where Kitty and crew had provided the notion, his heart had provided the emotion.

He had fallen in love with Mary van Doorn.

She winked at him, a sly, teasing wink. "Of course I don't want to marry you. Why would I?"

"I—well, I—"

Reaching across the table, she put a soft hand over his. Static electricity zipped up his arm. He refused to think it was anything more than that.

"Jake, if I weren't so unhappy with my friends over their shenanigans, I'd be thinking more clearly. You didn't go along with Bert's suggestion, did you?"

"Of course not!"

"Then quit looking so worried." She smiled reassuringly at him. "You're safe from me."

They shared a long glance, Jake feeling caught by the sweetness in her pretty eyes.

Then she removed her hand from his. "What do you say we let you look over Sunflower Acres? You need to inspect every room in the house and the grounds if you want to make an offer."

Oh, he was starting to think he wanted to make an offer, all right, but it had nothing to do with Sunflower Acres. It had nothing to do with the town being named after him.

It was Mary, plain and simple. Suddenly, he had a burning question searing his mind.

If he asked her, *would* she marry him? Or not?

MARY WAS FURIOUS with Bert for the marriage proposal which had obviously been foisted upon Jake. Poor Jake looked as if he'd been caught in barbed wire! Fortunately, truthful Cruise had been worried about her interference in his life and had spilled the beans.

Tomorrow morning she would have a serious talk with her good friends. Her too-well-meaning friends. She had to explain to them that their intentions were good, but their method was not.

Tonight was business. As Jake helped her into his car, she kept that in her mind. Tonight was only business.

Jake liked her well enough, but he was not in love with her. She was falling in love with him. The pain she felt over the dismay she'd seen in his eyes made her feel cold inside. Lonely. Like the wallflower at the school dance.

"Miss Mary?" Cruise asked from the back seat where he was strapped into his booster chair.

"Yes?"

"Can I make one of those houses again? For the birds?"

She smiled to herself. "I've got a new project to show you."

"Okay."

Jake reached over and patted her hand gratefully. But she didn't smile at him.

It really wasn't his gratitude she wanted.

TEN MINUTES LATER, they pulled past the cheery welcoming sign at her farm. Mary got out of the car and opened the back door so that she could get Cruise out of his seat. Taking him by the hand, she intended to get him busy with his "project," but Esther stalled her by coming out onto the porch.

"Hi, Mary! Hi, Jake!" Esther walked over to meet them. "Hello, Cruise. How are *you* today?" she asked in a happy voice to make him feel welcome.

He stuck a finger into his mouth. "Fine."

Her sister straightened and met her gaze. "I'm going over to Miss Kitty's, unless you need help with something."

"I want to see Miss Kitty," Cruise asserted.

They all three stared at the boy.

"I thought you said Bert talked to you guys at the Shotgun?" Mary looked at Jake. "Didn't Kitty say hello?"

"Actually, no."

She wondered at Jake's concerned expression. Instantly, she realized he was hiding something. More had gone on while she was hiding in the ladies' room than she'd guessed.

"Can Cruise go with me to visit Miss Kitty?" Esther wanted to know.

"No," Jake and Mary said at the same time.

"I want to!" Cruise wailed.

Mary didn't want to be alone with Jake. She knew most definitely that it would be hard to keep on "business" without the little boy around as a protective shield. With the twilight falling and the temptation of Jake, she might want him to kiss her. Hold her.

Jake didn't want to be alone with Mary. All he needed was one flimsy excuse to touch her, and all his gentlemanly aspirations would turn to dust. He wanted to touch her and feel her against him.

Cruise couldn't leave him.

"Please, Uncle Jake?" His nephew stared up at him with hopeful eyes.

Esther laughed. "They've moved the domino game to Kitty's house tonight, and I'm taking over some brownies for refreshments." She smiled at her sister. "I'm so looking forward to living with Kitty, Mary. I'm glad you agreed for me to stay here in Sunflower."

Mary swallowed tightly. She had known all along that Esther didn't want to leave. Thank heavens for Kitty! Though she was still put out with Kitty's pursuit of matrimonial bliss for her, she couldn't deny that the elderly woman had always been heaven sent. "I just want you to be happy. Kitty is an angel."

"Well, can I take Cruise with me?" Esther asked Jake. "We won't get into any trouble, I promise."

The three waited anxiously for his reply.

"I guess so," Jake said begrudgingly.

"Yes!" Cruise gave a little hop of joy.

"Mind your manners at Miss Kitty's," he instructed a bit more sternly than he'd meant to.

"I will."

"Mind Miss Esther."

"I will!" He hurried after Mary's sister, his little feet scrambling as they walked toward the family truck.

Esther and Cruise might not get into any trouble, but she hoped she could say the same tonight. While he watched his nephew go, Mary allowed herself one slow, longing glance from the top of Jake's head to the boots he wore with his well-fitted jeans and indigo-blue shirt. He filled out his clothes so nicely! It was rare that she met a man she had to look up at. Jake made her feel dainty, feminine.

Esther and Cruise waved gaily from the window as they drove away. "Goodbye!" they called.

"Well!" Mary said. It suddenly seemed terribly quiet with Cruise gone. Determined to stay on a strictly business agenda, she asked, "Shall I show you the house?"

"All right."

She noted his relief at her brisk attitude. Jake was no more eager to fall into a trap of them being alone than she was. They walked into the house together, with Jake holding the door open for her. He closed the door and suddenly Mary couldn't stand the formality and the pretense any longer.

"Jake? Why didn't Kitty come over and say hello to us while we were at the Shotgun?" She paused, watching him carefully. "It's not like her not to attach herself to Cruise. And vice versa."

"Well…" Hesitation showed in his deep blue eyes. "I guess Bert had been elected to be the spokesperson. As the mayor of Sunflower."

None of that made sense. Mary frowned and shook her head. "Why did Bert need to speak to you in an official capacity?"

Jake appeared uncomfortable. "Let's just do the room tour, okay?"

There was definitely something he did not want her to know. "Whatever it was, I'd like to hear it from you," she said softly. "I won't hold you to whatever it is that they've come up with this time. I promise."

He looked disgusted. "It's not that! I just don't

want to get into it. My mind is on buying your house.''

''I think I should know, Jake.''

''Oh, for crying out loud,'' Jake complained. ''Mary, I know you well enough to know you're going to be mad when I tell you what their latest scheme is. So can you just trust me? This is one thing I'd rather not get into.'' His gaze fell on her lips, hesitating. ''Especially when there are so many other things I'd rather do than argue.''

With unyielding intent, he pulled her into his arms. She didn't need a whole lot of pulling to get her up against his body. After all, it was exactly where she wanted to be.

''I'd rather do this,'' he murmured, touching his lips to hers.

She closed her eyes, sighing inside as the kiss deepened. Sliding her hands along his shoulders, she massaged him, wishing there was no cloth between her fingers and his skin.

''And this,'' Jake whispered huskily, moving his lips to blaze a trail along her neck. Mary felt a sigh start inside her body and send a shiver all over. Tingles of excitement ran up her arms. She moved her hands tentatively down his back and toward his waist, exploring his physique. Every inch of him felt so good! She rested her head against his chest as he nibbled on her shoulder.

''Jake?''

''Yes?''

He stroked the sides of her dress where her bra lay underneath. Mary thought she would jump out of her skin. ''Please tell me. As wonderful as this is, I don't want to do it knowing that you're keeping something from me that will upset me. It just doesn't feel right.''

He sighed, tipping her chin up so that he could look down into her eyes. "Promise me you won't get mad.''

"I promise.''

"Because if you do, I'll have to exact extreme measures,'' he warned her with a smile. "I refuse to let Kitty and crew's plotting spoil my time alone with you.''

"I won't.'' She stared into his eyes, almost hypnotized by her feelings for him.

"If I marry you and settle down in Sunflower Junction, they propose to name the town after me.''

Mary's chin dropped. She jumped away from Jake. "*What?*''

He advanced on her. "You promised,'' he reminded her.

"Oh, no. No, no, no!'' she exclaimed. "I have every right to be angry!'' Holding up a hand to ward Jake off, she moved behind the sofa so he couldn't get to her. "That's despicable, Jake!''

Chapter Eleven

"Despicable, *Jake?*" he demanded as he followed her around the sofa. "I didn't have a thing to do with it. And you assured me you wouldn't take this out on me. I feel very much that I'm bearing the brunt of something I had no part of."

She refused to be drawn back into his embrace, though he'd caught her hand. Jerking back, she hurried to the opposite end of the sofa. "You're not exactly bearing the brunt. But I don't think I can be blamed for not feeling like kissing when I've been offered in trade for a town name!" She walked around the sofa arm and sank into the cushions. "Ugh. That sounds awful!"

Jake slid next to her. "I think Maddox, Texas, sounds kind of, I don't know...it might grow on you."

She tried not to laugh and ended up with a sigh of amused disgust. "Too bad you lose out on that particular door prize. I'm going to have a serious talk with Kitty. And Bert. And Tom and Swinnie. Mr. and Mrs. Butt-in-ski are top on my list. Official capacity as mayor, indeed!"

"They're just looking out for you—"

"And as I've told you before, I can take care of myself!" She stared at him. "Where do you stand in all of this? Are you kissing me to get a town named after you? Is that heavy stuff for the male ego?"

"No!" He reached over and tugged on the decorative buttons that marched up the front of her dress in a prim little line. "I'm kissing you to get this dress off you. Oh, these don't come undone. Pesky little things put there to trick a man into making the wrong moves."

"Jake!" She laughed and smacked his hand away.

"What? I'm a guy, aren't I? I do have ulterior motives." He sneaked a kiss to the side of her neck and ran a hand around her waist, fitting her tightly to him. "They have nothing to do with town names, however."

Her breath caught as he moved his hand across the cotton waist of her dress. "What did you say to Bert's offer?"

He ran one hand through her long hair, tugging it so that she had to tilt her head. "That I'd think about it," he murmured, kissing her nose, then her lips in a teasing descent toward her neck.

She tried to push him away. "You did not!"

"Yes, that's precisely what I told him." He flicked one of the tiny buttons at her waist with a careless finger. She jumped, and he flicked the next one up.

"Are you thinking about it?" she asked, her eyes wide at his audacity for his answers and the way he was sabotaging her dress.

He gently flicked the button just under her bra closure. "I'm thinking about you."

She stilled as he moved his hand smoothly over her breast. He gazed into her eyes. "Are you thinking about *me*?" His voice was a husky question as he kissed her long and deeply, his finger lightly teasing her nipple into a hard peak just as he'd toyed with her dress buttons.

A small moan of delighted anguish escaped her. She moved her hand up his chest, nearly dying of mortification when her fingers ran across the two buttons at the collar of his shirt. They felt hard to her fingers, just like her nipple must feel to him.

"Oh, Jake," she murmured, pulling slightly away from him. "You make me feel so...hot." Shyness overcame her at her bold words.

"Do you like that?"

"I think so." It was hard to look at him with the hunger in his eyes. But she liked knowing he wanted her. "I think I like a lot about you."

"No drawbacks?" He quirked a teasing brow at her and moved his hand from her breast to her shoulder, making her feel like she was released from a sensual prison she hadn't really wanted to escape.

"None except for your collusion with my friends," she shot back.

"You know, my mother would be thrilled to have a town with the family name. She'd brag endlessly at cocktail parties." He inched her ankle-length, ballerina-waist dress up, moving a warm palm over her knees, and Mary thought she would jump through the roof. She kept her legs pressed tightly together.

"Are you seducing me?" she demanded. "Because if you're trying, I've got to warn you that I'll be certain you're falling in with their bribery. And that won't endear you to me at all!''

"Mary," he said, sliding his hand tantalizingly up to her thighs, lingering as he stroked the soft skin, "I came out here tonight to make an offer on your property. I haven't even seen your fields." Inclining his head, he suckled lightly on her bottom lip for a fast second before letting it go. "Or one room of this house past the kitchen and dining areas."

She stayed very still, not sure what he was up to, but knowing it felt wonderful.

"Should I make an offer on a property I haven't inspected?"

"No," she barely managed to reply.

"Maybe I should inspect you thoroughly before I decide whether I can be bribed." He ran one finger up her back along the zipper of her dress, making it rasp and making Mary straighten like a stick. "I might change my mind about Bert's offer. I like the goods so far."

"Jake!" Mary jumped to her feet. "You're teasing me! And you're seducing me at the same time!" She stamped her foot. "Make up your mind! I don't think I can handle both at once!"

"Why not?" He stood to pull her into his arms.

"Because it's not organized. It's either one or the other but surely not both."

"Oh, Mary," he said with a mischievous smile, "I like blowing your skirt up." He whipped the back of her long skirt up with one hand while he held her against him with the other.

She shrieked and tried to snatch it back down but

he held it tight in his hand. "Jake, put my dress down!"

"I can't," he said, suddenly puzzled. "The lace is caught in my watch band." Removing his hand from her waist, he started to undo the hem from where it had gotten trapped. Halting, he said, "I kind of like this, actually. Your dress is up, you're stuck against me, I can take advantage of this sudden exposure—" he ran a hand down Mary's spine and over her posterior, eliciting a tiny slap on his shoulder "—Is there a reason I should release you?"

"So I can get away from you," she said, not meaning it a bit but deciding she wanted to see what Jake would do in the face of her threat.

He released the hem lace. The material fell once again to her ankles.

Mary didn't move.

Neither did Jake. But he did grin at her. "Is it my teasing or my seducing that keeps you a prisoner in my presence? Or my ability to charm you in spite of my disorganized approach?"

"What was your answer to Bert?" She had to know. She couldn't go one touch further, one layer deeper in her heart, until she knew how Jake really felt.

He took a deep breath, seating himself on the sofa again and reaching up to pull Mary down into his lap as if she were not even as heavy as a china doll. "I told him you were your own woman. That you had your own dream. And that while I knew they were trying to see to your happiness, you wanted something different." He paused to see how Mary was taking his words, but she waited to see if that was all he would say. "And then, because I didn't want to hurt his feelings, as I can't help being very struck by how much they care for you, I said I'd think about it. I'd keep his offer in mind and consider it." He picked up her fingers in his hand and kissed the tips. "Mary, I know it's hard not to be frustrated with them, but from the other side of the tracks, I have to tell you that it's really difficult when no one cares about you at all. When no one gives a damn about your best interests."

He was talking about his mother. She thought about poor little Cruise, confused about his place in the world. He reached out to Kitty and Esther, then pushed Mary away because he didn't want to give up any of Jake, who was the first person who'd shown him love in his young life. Instantly, she knew she was looking at the face of a grown-up Cruise as she stared into Jake's eyes. "Thank you," she whispered, her heart wringing inside of her.

"For what?" He stared into her eyes, never letting go of her fingers as their hands lay entwined in her lap.

"For helping me to see them another way," she said softly.

They sat quietly for a few moments. The mantel clock ticked softly, brushing seconds by with its whispery rhythm. Mary laid her head against Jake's shoulder.

"A lesser man might be intimidated by them."

"I am in no way a lesser man."

She looked up. "Are you boasting or hinting?"

He snorted. "Neither. Just stating that Kitty and crew won't run me off." Jake smoothed his palm up and down the length of her arm, stroking. "It was great of you to tell Cruise he could marry me when he grew up, Mary. I was intent on straightening him out. Then I saw how happy it made him to think he could and I realized I hadn't understood he was really looking for security."

A small smile flitted over Mary's lips. "I wanted to marry my mother when I was little. I thought she was the most wonderful person in the world. My kindergarten-aged friends tried to tell me I couldn't marry a girl, and I sure couldn't marry my mother, but all I knew was that I wanted to stay with her forever. When I was a little older and figured out boys went with girls, I wanted to marry my dad." She laughed softly. "I was kind of jealous when I realized he was already taken. And by my mother, of all people. I felt excluded." Looking up at him, she said, "I think Cruise is pretty normal in that regard. Dreams are necessary to individual growth."

He kissed her temple. "Thank you for caring about him."

"I understand him being possessive of his handsome uncle. I think I would be, too." She gave him a wicked, warning smile.

"Do you think so?" He seemed fascinated by that.

"Scares you, does it?" Mary said, lightly flicking his shirt button.

"I'm not sure, but I don't think so."

She ran one finger down his shirt toward his belt. "Oh, I'm positive I'd be jealous and possessive if you were my man. And a shrew, and demanding, too. Lucky for you I'm going to California." She tapped his belt buckle the same way she'd flicked his shirt button.

"What would you demand?"

"Oh…" Mary shook her head at him, her gaze deliberately naughty. "Field chores with your shirt off, night-time back rubs, breakfast served to me in bed with you wearing only a linen napkin and me wearing only your boxers that I'd just removed—"

"Mary van Doorn!" Jake interrupted with hoarse surprise. "Are you teasing me or trying to seduce me?"

"Maybe both." She gave him a demure smile.

"Make up your mind, woman, because it's either one or the other."

She could feel a bulge rising underneath her hand. "Hmm, I still think maybe both."

"Mary!" he growled.

"I may be entering a phase in my life where disorganization holds some attraction." Lightly, she brushed her palm over the bulge in his jeans.

He grabbed her hand in his. His eyes glowed fire. "I wish you wouldn't enter it tonight. I don't think I can stand the temptation."

"Really?" She was pleased that he would be tempted by her.

"Really." He removed her hand from him and kissed it. "I don't think you realize what you do to me."

She dropped the teasing. "I don't think you realize what you do to me, either."

He sighed. "Tell you what. Let me skip looking through the house tonight. It would be risky to be alone in a bedroom with you."

"Yeah?"

"Yeah," he said gruffly. "I might have to toss you in a bed and ravish you."

"Oh, dear." Mary shivered. "*Ravish* me?"

"Oh, yeah. Definitely have my way with you." He nodded his assurance. "You're not quite ready for that."

"Oh, I might be."

"No. You couldn't handle it." He kept shaking his head.

"What?" Mary said laughing. "Why do I get the feeling it's you who's backpedaling here?"

"I can't stand it." He moved her off his lap and stood. "I'm only so strong. I vote we go raid the fridge or go out to eat or do something before this gets out of hand."

"Why, Jake," Mary said, getting to her feet to look at him, "I do believe you're afraid."

"I'm just relying on the watchword of a gentleman. Retreat is part of the code of honor when a lady's, uh, uh—"

"After your body?" She raised a brow at him. "When you've been bragging so shamelessly?"

He opened his mouth to answer just as the front door slammed.

"I'm home!"

Mary turned, frowning, toward the hallway. "Rachel?"

"Yep. It's me." She walked into the den, all disheveled from wind. "Hey," she said, extending her hand to Jake. "Excuse my appearance, please. I've ridden on a motorcycle through several states in the past few days."

"What are you doing home?" Mary demanded. Belatedly, she remembered to give her sister a hug. "I was about to mail some wedding presents people have sent you to your new address."

"No need now," Rachel said softly. "I'm home for good."

"Now wait a minute. Jake is here to put an offer—"

"Let that wait for another time, Mary," he interrupted. "Maybe your sister would like a glass of tea."

Mary hesitated. Her mind was racing a thousand miles a minute. Something had happened to make Rachel run off from her husband. They *had* married, hadn't they?

Rachel couldn't come home, properly eloped or not. Sunflower Acres had to be sold so Mary could go to California without leaving behind responsibilities.

She stamped that bit of selfishness down and allowed herself to see the pain and embarrassment in Rachel's eyes. "Of course you need a glass of iced tea. What am I thinking of?" Her gaze went guiltily to Jake. She'd been irritated by the hitch in her romantic evening with Jake! "Why don't you go wash up and change—I haven't packed your bedroom yet so you can still get to your clothes—and I'll fix you a nice snack."

"What do you mean, packed my bedroom?"

"To send your things to your new address." Mary realized Jake was right to keep off the subject of selling the house while Rachel obviously had a problem she had come home to solve.

"Oh. No need to do that now." She disappeared

down the long hallway toward the bedrooms. They could hear her sobbing.

"Oh, dear." Mary gazed at Jake, distressed. "The easy rider must have decided he liked riding solo. Thanks for stopping me before I made matters worse."

"No big deal." He followed her into the kitchen. "Maybe I should go pick up Cruise and head back so you can talk to your sister."

She sighed, terribly disappointed. "Oh, well, you were halfway out of here anyway."

"Meaning what?" He put a hand over hers as she filled the tea glass, forcing her to put it down so that he could turn her toward him.

"You know." She shrugged. "Watchword of a gentleman and all that."

"I was just..." He halted, staring into her eyes.

"I know. Looking out for my best interests." Sighing, she went back to setting out a tray. "Funny how people are always looking out for my best interests while they manage to need something from me."

"Mary!" Jake couldn't believe his ears. "You're not really mad, are you?"

"No." Picking up the tray, she headed out of the kitchen. "Just disappointed." She stopped as she went into the hallway. "Jake, do you mind showing yourself out? I think I'm going to be back here for a while."

"Ah, no."

Mary nodded, turning and disappearing into one of the rooms. The door shut behind her. Jake ran a hand over his chin, amazed at how fast Mary had gone from playful wanton to caretaker.

And she hadn't seemed too happy with him, either. Had she felt hurt that they didn't make love? He'd assumed Mary was only being innocently seductive, and he'd been trying hard not to grab her and make more of it than she might have meant.

In fact, he'd been making a Herculean effort to keep from turning that dress into something fit only for dusting furniture at Sunflower Acres.

He did want something from her, she was right about that.

But obviously she'd misunderstood his reluctance to poach on emotions he didn't think she had for him. And he'd ended up hurting her feelings by making her think he was "looking out for her," when maybe he was only interested in buying her house. Or perhaps having her help him with Cruise.

He had wanted that from Mary.

Rachel wanted Mary's comforting.

Kitty wanted Mary to get married so she could have her nearby—and surrogate grandbabies. So did Tom and Swinnie and Mayor Bert, in his official capacity.

The twins wanted advice for the lovelorn, now that they were in Dallas meeting men at engagement parties for Eve. Eve wanted help planning her wedding. Joan had called today to ask questions about course work. Esther wanted something from Mary, too, mainly to be left here in Sunflower Junction. She was a little more independent than the other sisters. More like Mary.

Even Cruise liked Mary's attention, though he wasn't about to admit it. But he'd been anxious to start another sunflower birdfeeder project with her, and that was a sign that gave Jake hope.

Mary was trying to pack up a house for all of her sisters and get herself off to finish her residency at the same time.

Jake headed out the door to Kitty's. Butt-in-skis maybe, but they could assist him with his plan. It was time to give Mary something *she* needed for a change.

Chapter Twelve

Jake's cell phone rang as he was on the way to Kitty's. "Hello?"

"Jake?"

His sister's teary voice brought a frown to his face. "Steffie? What's wrong?"

She sniffled. "N-n-nothing. Can I talk to Cruise?"

"I'm on my way to pick him up right now. What's going on?"

There was a long pause from the other end.

"Steffie?"

"What do you mean you're on your way to pick him up?" She sounded a lot less teary now but definitely more worried.

The sudden concern on her part was somewhat annoying. Jake negotiated a turn into Kitty's driveway. "He's visiting a grandmother-type he's taken a shine to." He thought that was the best way to explain it.

"I don't understand why you're not with him. Why have you left him alone with someone? Cruise wouldn't want to be left alone with a stranger."

Jake scowled. He could hardly say that was the case, though he could also see why Steffie would wonder. He'd had Cruise less than a week. Yet, he questioned the sudden concern on the part of a woman who'd put her small son on an airplane with no toys to keep him occupied and no companion in case he was frightened of his first plane ride. How did one explain that he felt Mary and Kitty and crew were more family to him than the family he'd grown up with?

"I assure you Cruise is adjusting well and is very happy," he said sharply.

A masculine voice came on the line. "This is Cruise's father. I want him. I'm filing a lawsuit to get custody of him from Steffie and the rest of you," the man snapped. "I suggest you don't leave my son with strangers anymore."

Jake's jaw dropped. The line went dead at the other end. He'd never envisioned Cruise's father. Steffie had never mentioned him in the three years since Cruise's birth. Jake had not wanted to know about him, assuming his sister had gotten pregnant by some teenage kid from her own set of school acquaintances.

The man who'd threatened him sounded older, mature—and determined.

Jake couldn't breathe for the shock. He had planned his entire future around Cruise, even to buying a house in the country where the child could run and play and learn about birds and plants. He had planned to move his office into his home so he could spend every possible moment with Cruise.

His heart felt as if it had just been torn from his chest.

Swiftly, he punched in some numbers on the cell phone.

"Hello?" His mother's cultured voice resonated in his ear.

"Mother, it's Jake."

"Hello, dear. Long time, no speak."

He closed his eyes, hating the false affection in her tone. "I can only talk a second, so I'll make this brief. I just got a call from Steffie and some scuz claiming to be Cruise's father. He says he's filed a lawsuit to get custody."

"I know. Steffie told me." There was considerable disinterest from the other end.

Jake took a deep breath. "Who the hell is he and where the hell has he been for the past three years?"

"I'm sure I don't know." The inference was that the conversation was distasteful to her. "It's Steffie's business."

"Wrong. It's your business, and it's my business, Mother. Get over yourself and pay attention. If he's filed a lawsuit, then all your friends are going to find out because it's going to become nasty and ugly. *Capisce?*"

"Why should it get ugly?"

"Because I'm not handing Cruise over to some bozo who hasn't made one phone call on his behalf since the day he was born!" Jake frowned at his mother's detachment. "Does that make sense?"

"Actually, no. That's Steffie's problem. It's her...um, boy. She doesn't want to take care of him, so why not let his natural father have him?"

"I don't believe it. Mother, you live in a dream world." He snapped the phone off and barely kept from throwing it out the car window. Getting out, he slammed the door and headed up Kitty's steps. He

rang the bell, and when Kitty opened the door with a
smile in her bright eyes for him, he could see past her
shoulder that Cruise was happily sitting at the table
eating brownies and drinking milk with Esther, Swinnie, Tom and Mayor Bert.

Tears stung his eyes as he remembered the sullen
boy who'd gotten off the airplane. *Oh, no. I will never
give you up without a hell of a fight,* he vowed silently. He managed a smile for Kitty. "I hope Cruise
has behaved."

Her eyes crinkled with delight. "Oh, he's no trouble at all. Not one single ounce."

"He's kept you busy, I bet."

"Well, Cruise isn't a TV-watching child, I'll grant
you. I turned on a Disney movie and he wasn't interested in that. So I had an old badminton set in the
garage we pulled out and played teams, boys against
the girls. Swinnie and I enjoyed watching those old
coots jumping around trying not to get swatted across
the shins." She smiled, her eyes kindly. "I reckon
badminton rackets are a mite long for Cruise to swing
effectively."

"I suppose you're right." He couldn't help smiling
back. Some of the intense pressure he'd been feeling
over Steffie's phone call released from his shoulders.

"Well, Tom and Bert are not as spry as they used
to be, Lord love 'em." She gestured for Jake to follow her into the dining room and take a seat at the
table. "So. What did you think of our proposition?"

He shook his head as he slid into a seat, not sure
where to begin. It was important that they know he'd
told Mary about it—and that she was none too
pleased with them.

"Uncle Jake, do you like brownies?" Cruise asked.

"Yes, I do."

"You can have some of mine," his nephew offered, holding out a square of chocolate between fingers which were coated with stuck-on brownie.

"I'll get Jake his own, but that's very mannerly of you, dear." Swinnie gave Cruise a benevolent glance. "He's coming along, Jake. Coming right along."

A painful lump settled in his throat. Best to stay off that subject for the moment, and stay on one that, while no less serious to the people in this house, required immediate attention. "I ended up mentioning your proposition to Mary."

"Uh-oh!" Bert intoned.

He had everyone's attention now. "I'm sorry," he told them. "But Cruise asked Mary if she was going to, you know. M-a-r-r-y m-e. He wasn't thrilled with the idea, and I had to explain how it had come up."

"We'll have to be more careful about little fountains of information in the future!" Kitty said brightly, ruffling Cruise's hair.

"So Mary might be a little annoyed with you all at the moment." He grinned broadly. "I apologize for divulging the plan, but if it's any consolation, I enjoyed trying to calm her down before Rachel came home."

"Rachel came home!" the foursome repeated in a horrified chorus.

"What do you mean?" Kitty demanded.

Jake hadn't realized how easy it was to sidetrack them. All they needed was another tidbit to stew over and they were in their element. "I don't know what happened. She came home upset and I left."

"I thought you were over here a mite earlier than I'd intended," Kitty murmured. "This presents a problem." She tapped her fingernails on the table. "Of course, maybe it presents a blessing. If Rachel's come home, then Mary can't sell the house, can she?" Quickly, she glanced at Jake. "I don't mean that we don't want you here, Jake. It's just that it's hard to think of anybody else living at Sunflower Acres."

"Oh, I understand." Best that Kitty work on a back-up plan now anyway, he thought dismally. Was it a good idea to buy an extensive property like Mary's if he was about to get locked into a fierce custody battle? The knot in his throat grew, making it impossible to eat the brownie Swinnie had placed on a paper-doily-decorated saucer in front of him.

"Well, I am at a loss." Kitty pursed her lips thoughtfully.

"I had an idea of my own," Jake admitted. "Although now I don't know that I can implement it."

"Strategy session! Everyone listen up!" Kitty commanded. Tom, Bert and Swinnie leaned forward anxiously.

Jake sighed. "Now I've got you all hopeful, and I didn't mean to."

"Just spit out your idea and quit leading us on," Tom demanded. "We're about running out of our own."

"I'd been thinking about taking Mary to California, since I knew you all were planning on driving her stuff out there." Jake frowned at the sudden approval shining in their faces. "I can drive one of those rented moving trucks."

"So what's the problem? You've got a drivers' license, strong muscles for moving furniture, and a quick mind for seeing the sense of jumping on our bandwagon," Kitty observed. "I vote yes."

"I was trying to give something to Mary," he said slowly, thinking about his part in wanting things from her. After holding her tonight, he just wanted that much more. "Making it easier on her to move her things out there seemed like the right thing to do." He sighed heavily as he glanced at Cruise. The boy was immune to Jake's dilemma as he drained his glass, leaving a milky smile widening the corners of his mouth. "Bert, I know it's a lot to ask, but can you take Cruise outside for a second? There's something I have to tell everyone, but I need to do it privately."

Bert and Tom got up together. "Little guy, how about we go skeet-hunting?"

Cruise hopped down from his chair immediately. "What's a skeet?"

"Well, it's a little bird kind of thing you only look for at night. They're so small you can barely see 'em, and they're tricky at hiding, too."

Jake listened to the tale while the men walked from the room. No one had ever taken him skeet-hunting when he was a boy. He longed for that kind of imagination game with Cruise.

"I got a phone call from my sister as I was driving over here," he said, his throat so tight it made his voice sound harsher than he'd meant it to. "Apparently, Cruise's father has shown up for the first time."

"Uh-oh," Swinnie breathed.

"Oh, dear." Kitty stared at him, her eyes no longer twinkling but terribly earnest.

"He says he's filed a lawsuit for custody of Cruise." Jake lowered his head so they couldn't see the sudden tears that sprang into his eyes, surprising him. They burned like fire.

Kitty's cool hand covered his, which he hadn't realized was on the table, fingers locked in a fist. Swinnie drew his other hand, which lay flat on the table as if he were steadying himself, into her own.

"We're glad you told us, Jake," Kitty said soothingly. "Mary doesn't know?"

He shook his head. "I finished the call in your driveway. The guy took exception that Cruise wasn't with me, that I had left him with strangers."

"Now, then, that's calling the kettle black," she murmured. "Never you mind about that. But I see why you can't go to California right now." Her tone was so comforting that Jake was lulled for a second.

"Unless you take Cruise to California with you," she said, so softly he barely heard the focused determination in her voice.

He raised his head, his eyes wide as he stared at her. To the left, Swinnie nodded her head in agreement.

"The sooner the better, to my mind. It delays delivery of any papers which may or may not have been filed," she continued blithely. "Of course, one never knows with fortune hunters. They threaten, they blackmail, but they very rarely follow through with legal documentation." She shook her frosted head. "Takes too much effort, and there's usually something they can't risk popping up on a background check *some* lawyers do as a matter of standard procedure. Bad checks, for example. Petty theft. History of jail time. Not that I'm suggesting you have a private detective do a thorough background check of the father in the least, mind you.''

She stared at him penetratingly, her water-blue eyes steely.

"You're damn good at this," he said slowly, realizing she was drawing a very large picture for him. "I didn't think of anything but what losing Cruise…" His mind ran through the possibilities she had illuminated. "I don't believe I've ever met anyone who could scheme on command. I'm very grateful for your suggestions."

Kitty patted his hand. "I was a huge fan of General MacArthur's during the war."

"And she adored the hell out of Bear Bryant later on, though he was coaching the wrong team, bless him. We could have used him in Texas." Swinnie squeezed his fingers in hers. "You just let Kitty work with you on this and you'll feel much better."

Jake felt strength flowing into him from the two women clutching his hands in theirs. His chest eased to normal again; the breath he'd been tensely holding left him in a sigh. "Fortune hunter?" he repeated with a puzzled frown at Kitty.

"Are you not a Maddox? Whose grandfather made his fortune in railroads? Whose father staked his claim in specially outfitted yachts?" Kitty inquired.

"Who told you that?" he demanded sharply. He wasn't close to his family so he never mentioned them. Never.

She nodded at him sagely. "I know an excellent lawyer and a gumshoe more than worth his salt."

"You had me investigated," he alleged, astonished.

"Would you expect any less of me where my godchildren are concerned?" she shot back. "Matchmaking without appropriate preparation is foolhardy."

They stared at each other for a long moment, assessing what her revelation meant to their growing friendship.

"Forgive me?" she asked, raising her chin at him stubbornly.

Somewhat dumbfounded, and yet questioning if he should even be surprised where Kitty was concerned, Jake shook his head in amazement. "Strangely, I do." It was the honest truth, though he supposed he should be angry. Yet he knew how she felt about the van Doorn girls, and it was second nature to her to protect them fiercely.

"Then allow me to give you a couple of names and phone numbers, unless you have your own counsel you prefer."

"I think I'd better use yours," he replied, still stunned. "I'm throwing in my lot with the winning team."

The two old ladies grinned at him hugely. "You'd better believe it," Kitty agreed. "I suggest you leave tomorrow."

"Tomorrow!" Jake's jaw sagged. "But…Rachel just came home. Mary won't leave her."

"We can take care of Rachel," Kitty assured him. "Broken hearts are our specialty."

"I—" He halted, staring at her in case she had a hidden meaning, but she appeared blithe with her remark. "I know she'll insist on being here for Eve's wedding."

"She can fly back." Swinnie's tone was as determined as Kitty's.

"Slow down for just a second. My brain's whirling." Jake jammed a hand through his hair once, and then again. "You're not encouraging me to kidnap my own nephew, are you?"

"Absolutely not. I'm simply suggesting you remain a moving target in case the cad *has* filed papers." Kitty took her hand from his and pushed the brownie he hadn't eaten closer to him. "And it might be best if you spent the night with Mary tonight."

"Oh, no, I'm not falling for that trick," he assured her. "I see exactly where you're going with that one."

"She means spend the night *at* Mary's," Swinnie said kindly. "Did you know Sunflower Acres has a reputation for being one of the finest, most popular bed and breakfasts in Texas?"

"I thought you said he probably wouldn't file papers." Jake crossed his arms. "So there's no need for me to remain a moving target."

"In the best-case scenario that would be true. But I'm not a mind-reader. In the worst-case scenario, he has or will follow through on this. Depends on how much money he thinks he can get by pulling this stunt." Kitty shrugged and poured herself some milk.

"So you think he doesn't want Cruise but hopes I'll pay him off?" Jake would pay anything to keep his nephew. He hadn't thought through the fact that perhaps the boy's father was bluffing.

The doorbell rang and Mary poked her head inside the door.

"Mary, dear!" Kitty crowed with delight. "Do come in and have a brownie."

Mary and Rachel entered the room, Mary avoiding Jake's eyes after meeting his gaze for only a split second. The elderly ladies jumped up and hugged Rachel. "Oh, you poor dear!" they cried, fussing over her.

That left Mary standing with Jake, who'd risen at their arrival. "Where's Esther?" she asked, glancing around the room.

Jake frowned. He'd forgotten all about Esther, though she'd brought Cruise over here tonight.

"She went visiting a friend. You know, girls have an awful lot to plan for Homecoming." Kitty glanced up from hugging Rachel. "Speaking of plans, Mary, Cruise and Jake need to stay in one of the guest cottages tonight. Jake, we're going to take Rachel back here for a minute and help her freshen up her face. You bring Mary up to speed."

That put him squarely in the hot seat, Jake thought, staring into Mary's eyes which had gone wide. "Uh, they're at it again."

"So I guessed."

"I didn't know you had guest cottages. Guess I should have looked over the property more closely."

"We have two. And yes, it would be wise to see everything before you make up your mind. Some guests we put in the house, but we try to keep the larger families out in the cottages for the sake of noise level and their privacy." She drew a hand through her long hair, as if she were nervous.

"Can you rent me a guest cottage?"

"You don't need to pay for anything," Mary said softly. "What has Kitty cooked up for you now?"

He sighed. "She's actually trying to help while getting us closer together at the same time. I found out tonight that Cruise's father has decided to threaten me with a lawsuit for custody."

"Oh, my gosh!" Her lips parted with dismay. "Jake, I'm sorry!"

Shrugging, he said, "Kitty believes I should stay where I can't be reached. I could take him into Dallas to stay at a hotel—"

"Absolutely not!" Mary vetoed that with force. "Kitty is right in this instance. I want to help. Besides, as a possible future owner of Sunflower Acres, you might as well try it out. Maybe I'll get an offer out of you." She finished that statement with a teasing smile.

He only hesitated a moment. "I have an offer for you. Mary, let Cruise and me drive you to California."

Chapter Thirteen

"Jake, that's so thoughtful of you," Mary murmured. Her heart spun crazily inside of her. There was enough to occupy him with the threat from Cruise's father; she knew how it would tear Jake apart to give Cruise up. Yet, he wanted to take her to California.

Suddenly, Mary knew that their relationship had gone way past prospective home buyer/home seller. For some incredible reason she couldn't even fathom, handsome, strong, wonderful Jake Maddox was truly interested in *her*.

And she was more than interested in him. As a medical doctor, she'd noted her racing pulse whenever he was near. She'd noted the flushed tingle that flooded her skin, but been too insecure to do anything more than ignore her own note-taking. In this moment, she allowed herself to recognize the signs for what they were: she was in love with Jake.

"It's not thoughtful," he said brusquely, pulling her into his arms as he moved into the parlor. "It's selfish and I have big-time motives. Don't see me as good when all I want to do is make love to you."

"Really?" She glanced up into his eyes, astonished.

He caressed her forehead with his lips. "Yes. I've been trying to figure out how to get your dresses off you for days."

"You haven't tried very hard." She felt safe pointing that out now that they were in the privacy of the dimly lit parlor.

Snorting, he ran a palm along her side toward her breast. "I am trying to live up to the gentlemanly image you have of me, but it's getting damn difficult. You're so soft, Mary." He buried his face in her hair, tugging at the ends that teased her waistline.

"You're not soft," she said in wonder, feeling hardness protruding against her belly.

"No."

She closed her eyes. "Jake?"

"Hm?"

"I think it's a wonderful idea for you to stay in a guest cottage tonight."

She met his gaze, her eyes full of meaning as he raised his head to stare at her.

"You do." His voice was flat.

"Yes," she affirmed, her voice shy.

He ran a finger lightly under her chin. "You really don't need any complications right now, Mary. You've got your hands full."

"So do you," she shot back. "But the best advice I ever took was Miss Kitty's and if she says you should stay out of Dallas, then I think you should fall in gracefully with her plans."

That got a smile out of him. "All of them?"

She didn't smile in return. "Except for the one about taking me to California."

"I didn't consult her on that. It was my own idea."

She lowered her gaze. "Thank you, Jake. But... I've decided it's not the best time for me to go away." Her eyes traveled the slow, painful distance to his questioning frown. It hurt, her decision cut her like she could never have imagined. "It's just not a good time for my family to be left alone." Tears burned her eyes. "If our parents were still alive, they could handle everything and I could go off freely, the way I always have." She took a deep breath. "The fact is, they're not here—so I will be."

Jake shook his head. "Just a second ago you offered me a place for the night so that as a possible future owner of Sunflower Acres, I could 'try' it out."

"Oh." She forced herself to fight the awkwardness stealing over her. "You're not the only one with ulterior motives, Jake."

He raised his brows, and she squirmed a little.

"Well, maybe I should be more forthright. I could have told you a long time ago that I wished I possessed the strategy skills of Miss Kitty so I could get you out of your jeans." She felt the stinging flush creeping up her neck. It seemed that even her eyelids tingled with mortification. "I didn't want to rush you."

He enfolded her in his arms. "I'll let you rush me any time you want."

She could feel his heart beating against her cheek as it lay against his chest. The sensation was amazingly intimate.

"But don't use me as an excuse to stay here, Mary."

Slowly, she leaned her head back so that she could see his face. "I don't think I am."

Blowing out a long sigh, he said, "Maybe you're not. But I don't want to get tangled up with all the other decisions you're having to make right now. I mean, for example, how do your sisters feel about selling the house?"

As much as she didn't want to, she admired him for questioning her reasoning. A couple of weeks ago she wouldn't have welcomed a relationship, not just as she was planning to leave for her residency. She'd fought Kitty's matchmaking tenaciously, always with her eyes on her goal. "Every single one of them has asked me to wait, despite the impracticality. On the other hand, they want me to finish my residency. So perhaps I'm not in the most practical frame of mind right now," she admitted. "Although I really do want to make love with you."

"Oh, I'm not asking for you to be practical, rational and sane when we do. I'm hoping you'll tear my jeans from my body, and my boxers and every other item of clothing I happen to be wearing at the time." He grinned at her wolfishly. "In fact, I can't wait. I wish I could take advantage of the distress you're suffering, because the thought of getting inside you is driving me crazy." He ran a palm lightly over her breast, then reached to cup her buttocks as he groaned. "I like you, Mary. I like you so much my mind leaves my skull when I think about you naked. I like you so much that the thought of you leaving just about kills me." He groaned again as he pulled the back of her dress up and caressed her bottom through her panties. "You need to leave Rachel's problems, and Esther's graduation year, and Cruise and I, back here in Sunflower Junction where it all belongs."

She was going to jump out of her skin if he didn't stop stroking her bottom. Her breasts were tight with desire; her breath caught in her chest so tightly she could feel her heartbeat thundering. He kept talking about her leaving, and all she wanted was his fingers to slip inside her so he could feel how much she wanted him. She clutched his shoulders, her fingers digging in.

"Ah, Mary, that's how I want you, when it's time," he whispered against her neck. "Wet, like this." His finger swept against her folds, back and forth against the smoothness. "And wanting me so bad, I know you're going to tear the skin from my back as I get deeper and deeper inside you."

"Jake," she moaned, half request that he stop torturing her with his words, half protest that he might stop the magic he was working on her body. Reacting instinctively, she moved against his finger, back and forth so that she was sure she was going to die. She reached to pull him tighter against her, squeezing his tight buttocks as she lost herself in the shattering emotions stealing over her. All of her shyness fled as she reached around to touch the hardness in front of his jeans. Her breath caught, and she moaned.

"You have to go," Jake said on a tight groan, "and I'd like to get you there."

He was taking her to wonderful places she had never been. Mary pressed her lips together, her eyes tightly shut as she massaged Jake through the rough material.

"Say you'll go, Mary. Say you'll achieve your dream. When you have, I'll know it's safe for me to ask for part of your life." His breath was warm and ragged against her hair.

She was about to come in his hand. His consideration for her excited her as much as everything he was doing to her. He panted harshly, reaching to squeeze her nipple as the hand in her panties stroked faster.

"Let me take you there," he demanded. "Say yes."

She was going, but she was no longer certain where. "Yes," she breathed. "Yes!" She climaxed powerfully, heat flooding out of her as if it were water into her fields. Sagging, she released herself to Jake, her heart thundering as she tried to get her breath again.

He slipped a finger inside her, and then two, sliding them in and out slowly, and Mary realized she was still a prisoner to Jake's spell. "Oh, Jake," she murmured, shivering with growing excitement. "I'm going to die." She clasped her fingers more tightly around his erection.

"I want you, Mary." Suppressed need made his muscles tremble. "But I'm a firm believer that anything worth having is worth waiting for." He arched as she reached inside his jeans to take him into her hand. "You're worth waiting for, Mary," he whispered hoarsely.

She couldn't reply. Leaning her forehead against his broad chest, Mary felt Jake, how hard he was, how big he was—and something blossomed inside her that she'd never imagined.

Beauty. Mary felt beautiful. He made her feel like a woman, wanted for herself alone. He made her feel powerful, because he respected her. Admired her for her studiousness and her goals.

And he desired her. He withdrew his fingers after stealing her wetness, breathing tightly as he held her body against his. He remained hard against her midsection, unsated. She knew what an effort he was making for her.

"Say you'll still want me when I get back," she whispered. "Promise not to change your mind."

He chuckled softly, nuzzling his lips against her hair. "I think, Mary van Doorn, you have very little to worry about on that score."

She tried to be satisfied with that, but it was the most empty feeling she had ever known. Because she knew that once she left Sunflower Junction, she would never come back here to live—and she knew that this was where Jake needed to raise Cruise. His dream for his nephew was country fields and quiet lanes and leafy tree houses, all those things a child should have.

Not the urban sprawl where she would join a thriving pediatric practice.

"You'll spend the night with me tonight?" she asked, her heart breaking inside of her because she already knew the answer.

He hesitated. "I think I'd better not."

She lowered her head in disappointment, although she knew why he wouldn't. He was afraid of what would happen between them, and he was determined to give Mary no reason to back out on her residency. If she hadn't wavered in her plans, he would have willingly spent the night. But he sensed her becoming overwhelmed with her situation. He was right. It would be a lot easier to throw in the towel and give in to her guilt than to leave it all behind.

"What will you and Cruise do?"

He shrugged. "Take Kitty's advice. Stay somewhere else tonight. Though I'm not sure what good it will do. Cruise's father could have papers served at my office just as easily. It won't be that hard for him to find out where it is."

"Oh, Jake." Her throat constricted with sadness. "I wish I could help you."

"There's nothing you can do. Don't take on one more responsibility, Mary." His eyes turned steely. "Everything will work out for Cruise and me."

It didn't seem right in the aftermath of their stolen moment that there was nothing he would accept from her. "Why won't you let me do anything for you?" she asked unhappily.

"Because," he said, kissing her fingertips, "you've already done more than you know for me."

"Be greedy, Jake," she whispered.

He laughed out loud as they heard Kitty and crew and his nephew spilling down the hall. "Believe me, I *am* greedy. I want it all." Smoothly, he eased her back into the living room so that it appeared as if they'd never stolen a sheltered moment alone. Mary glanced at him, memorizing his easy laugh and handsome features. Her body still tingled with unanswered longing.

If Jake Maddox thought he was going to get away

with a rush job like that, Mary told herself, he had another think coming.

"Jake, maybe you could rent the house for a year. We could see how both parties feel in 365 days," she slowly suggested.

"That's an idea." He hesitated, thinking it through. "Maybe it's an answer. I'd have to catch up fast on sunflowers."

"My sisters would come over to help harvest. And Kitty and crew."

"All right." He nodded, gazing at her. "You've got a renewable, 365-day deal."

"It sounds like such a long time," she whispered.

"It is sure as hell going to feel like it." He pulled her into his arms and they embraced for one last moment.

There was great security in knowing he would be around, protecting what she and her sisters loved.

Then he released her, and Mary stepped back a bit sadly. They'd keep in touch in the smallest of ways but it would have to do. Since he'd agreed to move into the house, there was no need to pack up her and her sister's lives. That was an enormous relief.

All of a sudden she realized Jake had set her free— he had proved to be more of a prince than Kitty could ever have imagined. He'd saved her from tearing up the happy family memories because they would still have their precious homestead.

Jake would take good care of everything she loved.

After he made it through the apparently inevitable custody battle he faced, she would thank him for putting her needs first.

Then she would pay him back in kind for not allowing her to satisfy his needs, although he'd made her feel like liquid sparkling crystal.

She could be every bit as determined as Jake.

THE NEXT DAY, THEY PACKED THE truck with Mary's suitcases, everyone's face morose and worried. Kitty, Swinnie, Tom and Mayor Bert acted jumpy, like summer crickets. Mary was sorry to dash their high hopes for her by leaving. Esther, Rachel, Eve, Juliet and Antoinette stood around the truck, having come to kiss her goodbye. Esther wanted to take Mary to the airport, so she slid into the driver's side and waited while Mary said goodbye to her family.

It was harder than she thought it would be. It had been terribly difficult to say goodbye to Jake and Cruise. Cruise had fallen asleep on Kitty's sofa while she and Jake talked until midnight. Then they'd left, and as a physician, Mary newly understood the meaning of a broken heart.

"You'll be all right out there." Kitty gave her a fast hug as she tried not to cry. "You be the best doctor California's ever seen."

"I'll try." Mary held back some tears of her own. "I know what you tried to do for me, Miss Kitty, and I do appreciate it."

Kitty smiled a little. "I know. You've always been a good girl. Contrary, but good all the way through." She patted Mary's shoulder and stepped away, her little face wrinkling up with unhappiness.

Mary looked away as she slid into the truck. They had no idea how it was tearing her apart to leave her family behind.

"Ready?" Esther smiled at her bravely.

Mary drew strength from her sister's determined smile. "Yes, I am."

"Good. Wave big, smile bigger and show them all that they're going to live without you," Esther said briskly as she pulled down the drive.

That made Mary laugh despite the stubborn tears which jumped into her eyes, so she leaned out and waved goodbye like mad. All her sisters and godparents yelled good wishes and blew kisses and before she knew it, Mary couldn't see them any more.

"That's that! You're free!" Esther cried cheerfully.

"Free! Then why do I feel like I've just done something wrong?" She stared at her younger sister with a bit of mystified irritation.

"Because you haven't stuck to your original plan." Esther glanced at her. "Has your plan ever failed you?"

"No."

"See? You've always known what you wanted, Mary. Don't feel guilty if other people have tried to distract you." Esther eyed the intersection traffic before shooting across faster than Mary liked. "I'm not going to let Miss Kitty distract me one iota. Now that you're gone, I know I'm next on her to-do list. So I've prepared myself."

"What do you mean?" Mary demanded suspiciously. Esther was her little sister, for heaven's sake. Though Mary needed a pep talk, she wasn't certain she should be getting it from her, nor was she comfortable hearing that Esther was "prepared" for Kitty.

Esther giggled. "Miss Kitty thinks that because I'm staying with her, she can keep an eye on me like a hawk."

Mary had thought the same thing. Her ears perked at this side of Esther she may have underestimated. "Oh?"

"She's been hinting for days about me staying off the water tower."

"Maybe it's a good idea," Mary said slowly. Things were so different when her parents were alive. They had all felt secure to indulge in occasional wild behavior. But that innocently capricious behavior held no attraction for Mary now as she felt herself slipping into a maternal mode.

"I don't think so!" Esther frowned as she gave her a sidelong look. "Mary, you're like a dark cloud. Don't clap your thunder around me. I'm not going to be the only van Doorn girl who didn't leave her mark on Sunflower."

Mary ground her teeth. "I'm not a dark cloud."

"You are. You used to be like sunshine. Now you're trying to rain on my parade—and everybody else's. For heaven's sake, if you like Jake Maddox so much, why don't you just change that part of your plan? Why don't you just ask him to marry you?"

Mary was dumbstruck. "I have no idea what you're talking about."

"You've been moping ever since the two of you said goodbye last night."

Had she been moping? "I did hate saying goodbye to him."

"Actually, you haven't been yourself for a while," Esther said with sibling meaningfulness, "but I wanted to see if you'd admit that Jake was the real reason you're sad to be leaving Sunflower. You were sure never sad before. Remember those days?" She shot her sister a purposeful glance. "You couldn't wait to blaze a trail out of here."

It was true. Mary had wanted to see the world. It sounded so impressive and exciting to be able to say that she was studying at Stanford University.

Why did it seem that she'd left her whole world behind now?

Esther patted her hand soothingly. "You'll be back in two weeks for Eve's wedding. Since you rented the house out to Jake and Cruise, he'll keep things running just fine, and before you know it, Christmas will be here."

Mary wouldn't be home for Christmas, of course. She had ER shift over the holidays and there was no way she could get time off. But Esther didn't know that. She thought that everything was going to be the same, and with youthful enthusiasm, went plowing on ahead in life. Mary envied her. She sat thinking until they reached the airport. Before she got out to take her bags from the trunk, she gave Esther a hug. "Don't let Miss Kitty keep you off the tower," she said mistily. "Enjoy your senior year. I'm sorry I've been such a wet blanket."

Esther returned her affectionate hug. "Don't be sorry. Just accept the fact that our folks did a good job raising us, and we're all going to be fine. It's nice of you to be concerned, Mary, but we're all old enough to make our own mistakes. And I have no intention of staying off the tower. I've got a plan, too. I've learned a lot from my big sister. Only my plan is outrageous, almost epic."

"It's comforting to know you have a plan. Actually, yours is more of a vision, and that makes me feel even better, somehow." Mary assured herself she wouldn't cry when she said goodbye to her baby sister and got out of the truck. "Just don't fall off," she instructed through the window.

"If I do, Jake can run me to the hospital," Esther shot back. "Isn't it nice to know he'll be looking after things?"

Mary didn't reply as a skycap took her bags from her. She waved goodbye as Esther pulled out of the unloading line, the family truck disappearing into the congestion of traffic.

Suddenly, she felt very alone. It was hard not to feel selfish, but she envied Esther's carefree approach to life. Had she ever been that way? It didn't seem so. She'd always been studious, with a plan that stood her in good stead. Mary sighed, and turned to show her ticket to the man at the counter.

A moment later, she was checked in. All that was left to do was find the gate. Disconsolately, she grabbed her large briefcase-style purse and headed upstairs.

In one of the shops, she bought a romance novel and a bag of chocolate candy. She stuck them in her purse and forgot about candy and romance. She walked to her gate and looked at the shiny airplane waiting outside the window which would take her back to the busy, hectic, yet comfortable life she'd known before her parents died.

"Hey, pretty lady," someone behind her said.

She whirled to meet Jake's broad grin. He carried Cruise in his arms, who, by the watery look in his eyes, was either crying or trying hard not to.

"Jake! What are you doing here?" She gave Cruise

a pat on the back since he seemed to be feeling down. His thumb was in his mouth and a worried look shadowed his eyes. But what she wanted to do most was shower kisses all over Jake's face.

"Coming to see you off. It's good luck to have a bon voyage party. I think it is, anyway." He glanced down at Cruise, his face concerned. "I didn't realize it would upset Cruise to come to the airport, though."

"Oh, dear!" Mary stared at Cruise. "What's wrong, honey?"

He nestled his face in Jake's shirt. "Don' wanna go."

She looked up at Jake, not understanding.

"I think he saw the airport and the planes and figured he was going h-o-m-e," Jake said over Cruise's head.

"Uh-oh." Mary's eyes widened as her heart went out to the little boy. If his father managed to get custody somehow, Cruise would be boarding a plane to return home, something he obviously didn't want to do. Jake and Cruise were bonded in a special way, Jake providing the love the child needed so desperately.

She peered up at Jake surreptitiously, understanding a lot of what Cruise was feeling. It was hard to leave his big strong uncle behind. "Cruise, you've just come to say goodbye to me," she said softly. "I have to go to California, but you're staying at the sunflower farm with your Uncle Jake, okay?"

He hid his face, apparently terrified that he might be removed from Jake's arms and somehow bundled onto the waiting plane. "I have candy, Cruise. Would you like some?'' She held the bag up to him, but even that didn't tempt him.

"Oh, Jake," she murmured. "It was really thoughtful of you to come see me off, but I think you'd better take Cruise home. He's so upset to be here."

She met Jake's gaze. He was staring at her, a warm expression in his eyes.

"We'll miss you," he said, his deep voice hitting a chord inside Mary which resonated with longing.

"I'll miss you both, too." She leaned to stroke Cruise's hair swiftly, before giving his head a quick kiss.

"Do I get one?" Jake demanded.

"Yes." She smiled slightly, standing on her toes to lean over Cruise and kiss his uncle. She kissed him very fast, but it still sent a shock running all over her skin.

"Come back," he told her.

"I will." Her gaze reluctantly went back to Cruise for a moment. "Good luck," she said, thinking about what Jake had in store for him with a custody situation. "I wish I could be here for you."

"It's going to be all right. I've got Kitty and crew on my side, and surely that's got to tip the balance in our favor."

She smiled wistfully. "It always has for me."

"Oh, that reminds me. Kitty sent your glasses. She says you might need them to see clearly."

"Thank you." Mary took the ugly glasses from Jake and slid them into her purse beside the romance novel. She hadn't worn them since she'd decided to take Kitty's advice and get contacts. It was a choice she hadn't regretted since she felt more attractive—and she wanted Jake to find her attractive.

He nodded. "Goodbye, Doctor Mary. I'm real proud of you."

"I'm real proud of you, too," she said softly. "Goodbye, Jake. Goodbye, Cruise."

Before she realized what was happening, Jake leaned over and stole a lingering kiss from her. It took her breath, and she was certain, the last remnants of her heart.

Then he strode away, still holding Cruise in his arms.

Mary watched until they melted into the crowd, then turned to board her plane.

JAKE MADE HIMSELF hold tight to Cruise for comfort as he strode away from Mary. This was a happy day, a big day which should be celebrated, and he wasn't about to spoil it for her. He needed to escape before he spilled the news which was breaking his heart.

Steffie was marrying her ex-boyfriend. The so-called father wanted Cruise that badly, apparently.

Jake didn't think he could give his nephew up. With Cruise's terrified reaction to seeing the airplanes today, he was totally convinced sending the boy away would be an irreparable mistake.

He had desperately wanted to confide his concerns to Mary. But he knew better than anybody that one more reason to stay would keep Mary in Sunflower forever. She deserved her dream. He wanted it for her.

He would face the gut-wrenching fear alone.

Chapter Fourteen

Kitty, Swinnie, Tom and Mayor Bert sat crouched over the barrel table in the bait shop, eyeing the dominoes less than enthusiastically. Mary had been gone for a month. They'd barely seen her for Eve's wedding. She'd had ER duty, so she'd flown in for the rehearsal dinner and straight back out the next night. She was so busy with her maid-of-honor duties that she barely said a word to anyone.

Kitty sighed. These past few years had been draining on Mary; residency was tough, crazy work. It was obvious Mary wasn't herself. She seemed tired, though cheerful for Eve's sake—in a forced way.

Kitty and Swinnie were just about run off their feet these days, too. With Esther staying with Kitty, she had plenty to keep her mind occupied. The school year had started, and there was always a friend or two popping over to plan Homecoming, or some other event, with Esther. So far, the water tower remained unpainted, and Kitty congratulated herself that at least her housemother skills couldn't be questioned.

Antoinette and Juliet were staying with Swinnie while Eve was on her honeymoon. For the sake of propriety none of the girls stayed overnight at Sunflower Acres, although they ran out to help Jake with the fields whenever they could. And Rachel floated back and forth between Swinnie's and Kitty's houses, depending on whoever had the most room. Kitty had seen Rachel's red-rimmed eyes, and though the girl hadn't said much about her med-student easy rider, Kitty was certain she needed to re-launch Rachel to help her get over that helmet-headed Romeo.

Trouble was, she wasn't certain if Rachel had married him or not. Eloping had been the mission—so had they? Kitty'd been too afraid of the answer to ask! How disappointed her dearest friends, the van Doorns, would be that Kitty had allowed one of their girls to ride off willy-nilly into the sunset to live in sin.

It made her suck in her breath with consternation, but she'd deal with that trauma later. Right now, the big, foremost emergency that had everyone down was the hearing date tomorrow for temporary custody of Cruise.

Kitty's powers of concentration were in a total knot. "I can't think," she muttered.

"I can't, either," Swinnie moaned. "There's got to be something we can do!"

"Shootin's too good for that man, coming in at the last second and acting like he wants Cruise," Bert intoned. "If I was a shooting man, I'd be mighty tempted, though."

"You just stick to fishing, Bert," Kitty snapped. "All we need to convince the judge to take Cruise away from us is you running around aiming a rifle!" She glared at Bert so he'd know to just sit on his barrel and be quiet if he couldn't make constructive comments.

Tom clicked his teeth thoughtfully. "Guess there's just nothing we can do about it," he said, his tone purposeful and challenging as he stared at the ceiling innocently. "Obviously, absolutely nothing. Zero, zip! In fact, our hands are tightly tied. We're prisoners of this fortune hunter's greed."

Swinnie gaped. "Tom!" she cried. "Don't challenge her, for heaven's sake! Especially when there's nothing that can be done. It makes her upset, and that's bad for her h-e-a-r-t," Swinnie spelled earnestly behind her hand, as if Kitty couldn't hear.

But Kitty's hearing was perfect—and the proper spur had been put to her. She jumped up to pace. They all watched her with hopeful curiosity.

"I've got it!" she cried victoriously. Clapping her hands, she stared at them supremely as they sat on their barrels. "Get ready, friends! The old brain hasn't failed to give up a good notion or two since it's resided in my head, and now is no exception." She gave them a majestic smile. "He doesn't know it, but Jake is about to get the family he always wanted!"

JAKE HAD NEVER been so afraid. There was no other word for it. He'd packed his and Cruise's bags quietly yesterday, then called to inform Miss Kitty that the two of them were driving to Austin for the court hearing since that's where his family lived and, more critically, where the case had been filed. Then they'd slowly driven toward their destination. Cruise had been quiet, as if he sensed Jake's preoccupation. He colored a book in the passenger seat, every once in a while glancing at his uncle. It would have been faster to fly, but that would have upset Cruise terribly, and Jake figured his nephew might be upset enough by the end of the day. So he drove, his mind humming as the miles and signs went by too swiftly.

Neither of them said much. Jake's mind raced with a thousand scenarios. Should he offer to pay Steffie's lover off? That smacked of bribery or something unlawful. So he'd played a waiting game, with the four elderly people on his side yet unable to do anything to help him.

Even his mother hadn't done anything to stop Steffie from cowing to her boyfriend's demand for custody. His mother knew damn well that neither she nor Steffie wanted anything to do with Cruise. His heart broke. If Jake never had a child of his own, this boy would be more than enough for him. He loved him like he'd never loved anyone in his family. In fact, Cruise had taught him the meaning and the sensation of love. His happy smiles, his boisterous energy, his rounded little body parts that never stopped moving, charmed Jake to the point that he thought his heart was being torn right out of his chest.

Surely the judge won't take him from me.

Yet he knew very well that birth parents were granted custodial rights more often than not. His stomach curled into a tight fist of painful pressure. Of all people, his mother could swing the balance, by telling the judge exactly how Cruise had been treated in her household. But his mother wouldn't do that, Jake knew, because that would let her social set know that she wasn't the nice, caring woman she portrayed herself to be, the philanthropist of all good causes. In fact, revealing herself as the social-climbing, self-absorbed woman she was would likely cut her out of the position she had been careful to cultivate. He had put in one last desperate, pleading call for his mother to impress upon Steffie that this proceeding was a mistake, that she would be harming Cruise—and that he'd already suffered enough. His mother had been cool to him, as always.

No, he could expect no help from her. Steffie was too thrilled to have her wayward boyfriend marrying her to stop and think about what was best for Cruise. His mother was too pleased that Steffie's behavior would be less socially humiliating.

The jaws of fear snapped at Jake, nearer now. Cruise put a small hand on Jake's leg as he stared up at him questioningly.

"Where are we going?"

Jake swallowed. "Austin." He hoped that short answer wouldn't invite more questions.

"Why?" Cruise cocked his head, his straight, shiny hair falling into one eye as he did.

I should have taken him to the barber, Jake thought irrationally. *Does Sunflower Junction even have a barber shop?*

"Because your mother wants to see you," he said slowly, hating to say even one word.

"Oh," Cruise murmured very quietly. "Do we have to go, Uncle Jake?"

Jake winced, scratching roughly at his neck as he thought that one through. How to answer? Truthfully, as much as possible. But he didn't want to upset the child. Still, he couldn't say Cruise wouldn't have to see her for long, or that Jake would take him to see

the state capitol when they were finished and later get
ice cream, because the reality was that Cruise and he
might not walk out of the courthouse together. Jake
could be driving back to Sunflower Acres tonight—
alone.

He needed a miracle. Fast.

THEY SAT IN THE FRONT ROW, in back of the lawyers'
tables and chairs, but where the judge couldn't possibly miss them. Four impossibly small, almost wiz-
ened elderly people wearing purposeful faces and
Sunday hats. Jake couldn't believe his eyes. Cruise
went ballistic with happiness, running down the aisle
to throw himself into Kitty's lap. Jake smiled as he
walked forward, his eyes stinging with unaccustomed
tears.

"My cavalry has arrived," he said when he got
near enough.

"We're not exactly cavalry, but we wouldn't let
you go through this alone," Kitty said briskly. "You
just keep your heart strong, Jake. You're going to get
through this."

He shook Tom's and Bert's hands before pressing
a kiss to Swinnie's and Kitty's cheeks. They all gave
him bracing pats on the back.

"I've never been so glad to see anyone in my life,"
he whispered in Kitty's ear as they exchanged a
longer hug.

"You're in a box, Jake, but if a character reference
from us means anything to that judge, then maybe we
can help get you out. Though I wish you had something more than four old people sitting on your side."

He glanced over to the other side of the courtroom

where his elegantly dressed mother sat with Steffie and some tall, ugly man who had to be her boyfriend. They looked away, pretending not to see him.

"I'd rather have you on my team than anybody," he told all four of them reassuringly. "I feel the odds aren't against me now."

They were, but maybe slightly less so. Jake would take it—gladly.

"Kitty!" a voice loudly cried. Everyone in the courtroom turned to stare as six young women dressed in pretty dresses filed down the aisle. Esther tried to look proper, then gave it up as she rushed forward to hug Jake's neck. Her sisters crowded around, hugging Cruise and Tom and Mayor Bert and everyone else in the courtroom it seemed. "How could you not tell me where you were going?" Esther demanded of Kitty.

"I left you a note on the table," Kitty said, her little mouth puckered with pleased shock at being overwhelmed by all the van Doorn girls. "You were out so late planning Homecoming that I couldn't tell you then, and this morning, I didn't want to wake you."

"What if my alarm hadn't gone off?" Esther cried. "I wouldn't have seen your note! We wouldn't have been here in time!"

Kitty's eyes filled with delighted tears. "I guess I didn't think you'd want to be here."

The six sisters stared at their godmother in horror. "Not want to be here!" Esther repeated. "Jake is family! Why wouldn't we want to be here for him and Cruise?" She shot a reproving glare to the people on the other side of the aisle who sat watching in astonishment. *"Family sticks together,"* Esther declared loudly enough for everyone in the courtroom to hear.

Jake's mother and sister snapped their heads back to the front of the room where they kept their gazes locked on their lawyers' chairs.

Jake grinned as the sisters began passing Cruise for kisses. "I sincerely feel the tide is turning in my direction," he told them. "I can't tell you how much this means to me. To us."

"Don't try to leave us out of something like this, Jake," Esther scolded gently. "We took you into our home. You're part of us now, and though you'll find us tough to get rid of at times, we don't turn our backs on one of our own. And Mary would have wanted us to be here." She gave Cruise a delighted kiss on the cheek. "Mary's done so much for all of us. This is a very small thing we can do for her."

"It's a great big thing to me," Jake said, accepting hugs of good luck from each of the sisters in turn.

"I know Mary wishes she could be here." Esther passed Cruise to Rachel and began ushering her sisters into the chairs behind the four elderly people. One by one, the sisters moved in to sit. The congregation on Jake's side of the courtroom was beginning to grow, he noticed with pleasure. In the beginning it had looked so grim to be just he and Cruise alone. Now there were six sisters in cheerful print dresses, two pillars of Sunflower Junction wearing hats of royal size, and two gentlemen—one a mayor—removing their fifties-style hats as the bailiff rose.

Jake felt the knot starting to tighten again, in spite of his unexpected cheering section.

At the last second before the bailiff opened his mouth to announce the judge, Jake felt a whoosh and smelled a sudden drift of perfume as someone settled into a seat behind him. He turned to look, his heart in his chest, and could only smile at Mary's pretty face as she leaned over the rail to kiss him quickly.

"I see you brought the hometown crowd with you. Kitty called me last night to say you would be here today. You should have told me," she remonstrated gently. "What a good boy you are," she said to Cruise, giving him a swift kiss as well before she headed to the second row with her sisters.

This started the kissing and hugging in the eleven seats—twelve now—the Sunflower Junction brigade occupied all over again as the sisters and Kitty and crew greeted each other as if they hadn't seen each other in ages. Jake heard Mary thanking her sisters for their effort on his behalf, and sentimental warmth burst into a blossom inside him. He grinned as he saw his mother, sister and her boyfriend glaring at the ruckus the sisters were causing. Surely he had everything he needed on his side now. He felt stronger knowing level-headed, wonderful, kind, sexy Mary was nearby. Her family had become his, and when this horrible ordeal was over, he was going to tell them all how much they meant to him.

"All rise!" the bailiff snapped with grim authority.

IT WAS A DAY Jake was destined to be unable to forget. He would live each and every agonizing moment over and over in his mind, from the moment the black-robed judge took his seat, to the moment he gave temporary custody of Cruise to his biological mother and father, and finally, to the exact stunning moment when Cruise was wrenched, crying hysterically, from his arms by the bailiff.

"You could do something about this." He turned to face his mother. Her stark eyes turned away from the plea in his voice reflexively. "You don't want him. You know you don't! They don't want him. Please tell the judge the truth!"

She said nothing as she turned to leave the courtroom. Steffie whirled at the last moment to whisper, "I'm sorry, Jake," before following. The biological father shot Jake a triumphant glare as he departed. Chills ran over Jake's arms as he listened to Cruise's wails fading as the distance between them grew.

He had never felt so empty in his entire life, until he felt Mary van Doorn slip her hand into his. Unobtrusively, but there she was.

God, how I need her.

Chapter Fifteen

"Are you all right, Jake?" Mary's quiet voice penetrated his shock. "I was going to take the last flight out of Austin tonight, but—I could change my plans if it would help," she said, her voice dwindling, lost in a shy appeal.

"You would do that for me?" Jake turned to stare at her, his expression angry and heartbroken.

"Yes," she whispered.

Kitty and crew and all the sisters crowded around to hug them and murmur conciliation to Jake. His heart was frozen. His body seemed stuck, unable to move. He heard their words, but not a thing they were saying. After a few moments, the hometown crowd melted from the courtroom.

He was left standing with Mary, whose big eyes stared at him calmly. Without question. He looked at her shining blond hair, her pretty ankle-length dress complemented by Mary-curves, and told himself to finally accept the healing she offered.

"I won't be good company," he warned. "I don't know if I can even carry on a conversation."

"Maybe we should get a six-pack so you can drink.

I'll drive. Or we could buy a vintage Led Zeppelin CD and blast our eardrums all the way home so we won't feel the urge to make small talk. Both might be called for.''

"All very intriguing suggestions from a doctor." Jake tried to smile, but his mouth was a harsh line that didn't quite turn up at the sides. "Not healthy, but intriguing."

"I'm a doctor, but I'm also human." She met his gaze. "Let me take care of you tonight."

After a long moment, he nodded. "You've been warned. If you're still interested, come on."

They walked to the parking lot. He opened the car door and she got in without hesitation. They didn't buy beer, they didn't buy a CD or play the radio, and they didn't say a word until they reached Sunflower Acres.

"I've missed you," Jake said.

Mary looked at him. "I've missed you incredibly."

"I wish that the first time we've seen each other in so long I was in a better mood."

She shook her head and put her hand on his forearm. "Let's go inside, Jake."

Silently, they walked in the house, their hands clasped together as they went into the den. "Are you happy here?" Mary asked.

"I was."

He had moved here for Cruise. Without Cruise, he wouldn't stay.

"I can't bear to hear the fight go out of you."

He stared at her.

She put her arms around him. "You'll get him back, Jake. You know that the good guy always wins,'' she whispered, before rising on her toes to press her lips to his.

"Who says I'm a good guy?" he demanded harshly, taking her face in one hand to keep their lips an inch apart.

"I do," she murmured.

She pulled his restraining hand down and made sure her lips stayed against his this time, denying his protest. He couldn't hold back any longer. Wrapping his arms tightly around her, he searched her lips for more than reassurance. A low moan escaped him. Mary moved against him, hinting in a feminine way that she wanted more than kissing from him.

"I'm not going to be a good guy much longer if you keep doing that," he stated without moving away.

"Maybe I should get to know your bad side." Mary ran her hands over his chest, flattening her palms over his shoulders.

"Maybe you shouldn't." He caught her wrists, stilling her hands. "I still think you're worth waiting for. I'll wait as long as I have to." Although the last thing he wanted to do was wait any longer. "It's like thorns on a rose. Maybe you have to work harder to get past the thorns to the sweet, soft petals, but it's worth it."

"This is a sunflower farm," she told him firmly. "No thorns around here."

"Yeah, but some of your sunflowers have damn bristly stalks. I've been very careful and patient with those."

"The wait is over. You promised me you'd still want me when I got back from California." She stared at him, challenge in her eyes. "I think it's time to prove it."

Jake couldn't deny himself any longer. He desperately wanted everything Mary was offering. He snaked his hand to the zipper in back of her dress. "I will." He jerked the zipper all the way down to where it ended at the top of her hips. Sliding his hand inside her dress, he felt smooth skin just above her panties. With his other hand, he undid her bra. "Don't do this because you feel sorry for me."

She shook her head at his rough tone, her eyes never leaving his. As she purposefully held his gaze, she pulled off the jacket of his suit. Then she undid the buttons of his business shirt one by one. She slid his shirt off. "The last thing I feel for you is sorry." She pressed light kisses over his collarbone, then trailed over to a shoulder. "It's not wrong to accept comfort, Jake. I want you to turn to me."

He slowly removed her dress, taking it from her shoulders and allowing it to drop to the floor. The bra he slid off more impatiently, his gaze intense as her breasts were revealed. "Oh, Mary," he murmured. She had beautiful breasts. She had a beautiful body. Everything about her was womanly and desirable. "I've got to turn to you. There's nowhere else I want to go."

Unable to do anything else, he lowered his head to capture a rose-colored nipple in his mouth. She buried her hands in his hair, pulling him close to her chest, and Jake allowed himself to fall freely into the kind of comfort she was offering. Hungrily, he laved her other nipple, squeezing one tip lightly as he suckled the other, enjoying her whimpers of passion.

She slipped his pants down and then his boxers, and he groaned when she took him into her hands. Gently, she massaged him, pulling his tight shaft upward with firm, repetitive strokes.

He was on fire. This woman wanted to be his comfort. This time, he was going to allow himself to appreciate her giving nature. "I've got to have you," he said hoarsely.

"I hope so. I know I can't wait any longer to have you." She lowered her eyelids for a second, before looking into his eyes again, waiting.

Lifting her, Jake carried her to her bedroom. Laying her on the bed, he took off her sandals, caressing her from her calves to her thighs. He dug his fingers into her soft skin for just a moment, commanding himself to slow down, before hooking his fingers into the top of her panties, drawing them down slowly as if he were unwrapping a Christmas present. Light curls were revealed, a slight covering of a tantalizingly sweet womanhood.

With a moan, he kissed the soft curls. Then he lightly licked the tip of her femininity. When she tentatively tried to push him away, he caught her hands. "I'm being greedy," he said. "I want all of you."

He licked her again, his tongue firmly pressing on her tip. She cried out with pleasure. Jake liked hearing Mary lose it like that. He did it again just to hear her say his name with such urgency and need. Then he slowly, tantalizingly entered her with his tongue, making sure she felt every satiny delight of his invasion. She grabbed at his shoulders.

"Jake! Please!"

"I'm going to please you. Relax, sweetheart."

Reaching up, he caught the roses of her nipples, massaging them and bringing them to a frenzied peakedness as he drew his tongue along her in one long, slow lap.

"Jake!" she cried.

"Okay," he murmured. Swirling his tongue, he felt the bud stiffening and her muscles contracting. He laved faster, teasing her nipples at the same time, and an instant later he had her gripped in the pleasure he wanted her to experience.

"Jake! Oh, Jake!" Frantically, she pulled at his shoulders as she gave herself up to him. Her pleasure made him feel like he was going to burst.

"You're so sweet, Mary," he told her, kissing up her belly toward her breasts as he covered her. Unable to wait a moment longer, he slid inside her, feeling a thousand sensations as he connected with the only woman he had ever felt this powerfully about. "So sweet that I want to consume every inch of you."

She locked her legs around him, and it felt like heaven as she rode him toward a whirling destination. Her hands tore at his back, pushing him deeper inside her, pulling him tighter to her. Closing his eyes, he groaned, allowing her to feel everything she wanted to feel as he stroked hard, fast, impatiently. When he felt her locking up again as she neared another climax, he strained to hold on. Mary's muscles tight around him were more than he could take. She cried out, going over a pleasurable edge, and he went with her as she called his name over and over and over.

He lay on top of her, stunned in the aftermath. Never in his life had he felt anything so strong. Her hands trailed lightly over his back, her body warm and accepting as he lay sated inside her. He felt as though he'd just released all of his worries, all of his cares. He was deep and connected...and comforted.

He didn't know how he would ever say goodbye to her again. Sweet Mary.

He wanted her forever.

AN HOUR LATER, Mary slowly awakened to find herself held tightly in Jake's arms. She lay against his broad chest, thinking she had never felt so complete. He ran one hand along her back aimlessly and Mary knew he probably hadn't slept at all. "I never knew it could be like that," she murmured.

He gave her a gentle squeeze. "Making comparisons? Or a general satisfaction comment?"

"No." She laughed. "I had one serious boyfriend in college, and even that wasn't very serious. Mostly we studied."

"I'm jealous." He tightened his arms around her. "I feel like I should hunt him down and kill him." Tugging her hair, he pulled her head back to look into her eyes.

She saw the laughter there. "If we're going to run around knocking off old exes, I'd require several more bullets in my gun than you'd need."

He shook his head at her, his gaze laughing. "You get quality points. You make me happier than any woman I've ever known."

"I do?" She wanted to believe him.

"Oh, most definitely. The woman you are is nothing short of incredible, Mary."

Her lips parted as she saw that he wasn't teasing anymore. He meant every word he'd just said. "I think I love you," she told him. "In fact, I know I do. Just for that statement alone."

He held her chin with one finger. "I knew I loved you when you came down the stairs wearing that sexy red dress and no specs just to please Kitty."

"You were laughing at me."

"I wasn't," he assured her. "I was falling in love. Against my better judgement, of course, but I couldn't help myself."

"Your better judgement?" She couldn't tell if he was serious or teasing now.

"Well, yeah. I mean, knowing you weren't going to be around long it was tough to want to fall in love." He leaned down to touch her lips with his. "You caught me, fair and square. The deed is done. I'll try not to be jealous, but it's going to be hard, Mary. If you were any other woman, I could maintain a very lukewarm relationship with you. But you're not any other woman."

She couldn't believe what she was hearing. "Maybe you're just in shock over losing Cruise."

He cocked his head. "Oh, so I didn't get custody of Cruise, kind of a lost-possession scenario, so I'll fill in with another warm body? That doesn't work, does it? There's no keeping you, my sweet Texas-bred, California transplant." His lips twisted wryly as he raised his brows. "Good thing you're a doctor, not a shrink. I'd get poor shrinkage for my money, obviously. Why is it so hard for you to believe that you're a mind-blowing kind of woman?"

She'd certainly never thought of herself in that light. She thumped him on the chest to tell him to mind his manners. "Now what happens?"

"I guess I...I don't know."

His expression was suddenly so unhappy Mary couldn't bear it. She tried to stroke away the pain in his face, but the lines stayed. He kissed her palm as she caressed his cheek.

"I think it's time for a new plan." She moved away from him reluctantly, but with purpose. "I've stuck to one plan all my life. It's been good for me. But it's time for a change."

He sat up, the white sheet falling to expose his strong, broad chest. Mary could easily see herself waking up to that every day.

"I like change," he said. "Sometimes. Although I will say that the other girls in the van Doorn household all change more than I'd be comfortable with. So don't change that much. I couldn't bear it if you took off on a nature-trail excursion with some long-haired med student."

"Hush," she told him. "I can't concentrate." Mary pulled on some jeans and a blouse, though Jake tried to swipe them from her. She tossed a blanket on top of him. "I assume you have plenty of clothes down the hall since you live here. Please put something else on besides that suit. It will depress me to the point *I'll* need a shrink."

"Are we going somewhere?"

He got up, ignoring the blanket. Mary's concentration shattered. Adonis in the bedroom she'd grown up in, where she'd dreamt wistful, ambitious dreams, was something she would never have wrapped her studious mind around. "Change is good," she told him. "At least it's going to be good. Wear something comfortable."

She gazed at the length of his body as he left the room to get clothes.

"I kind of liked you being a rock, Mary," he called down the hall. "I've been relying on you for steadiness amidst stormy waters."

"Oh, I'm still going to fully outline my plans," she yelled back. "It's just that I need to draw a bigger plan." Glancing around at the stuffed animals on the window seat and the gingham curtains at the window, she knew she was putting her childhood dreams behind her. She needed to sketch Jake and hopefully Cruise into her future—with indelible ink.

The phone rang, startling Mary out of her racing thoughts. She picked it up. "Hel—"

She broke off the greeting as she realized Jake had picked up at the same time, his baritone voice drowning hers out.

"What do you want, Steffie?" he demanded.

"I have to talk to you." The sound of crying penetrated Mary's surprise. Quietly, she hung up the phone and went into the room where Jake stood, half-dressed in faded jeans.

"I don't have a whole lot to say to you. You can tell me that Cruise is fine, but that's about all I want to hear from you," he told his sister.

Mary sat at Jake's motion that she do so. It felt good to know that he wanted her nearby while he had this obviously painful conversation.

A few seconds later he shook his head. "I don't care about Mother's problems. I don't care about what's-his-face's problems. I care about Cruise."

Mary watched the muscles in Jake's chest contract. She saw the tension cord his neck. How she wished there was something she could do! Quietly, she got up, going to Jake, where she leaned her cheek against his back, encircling his waist with her hands. He put one hand down and squeezed hers in gratitude.

"I don't think I'll be spending a million dollars to bail Mother out of her little problem." Jake's voice was stern, cold. "You tell your creepy boyfriend that if it's money he wants, he'd better look for it somewhere other than my wallet. He's not getting a damn dime."

Jake turned the phone off, putting it down on the table with a hard thump.

"So Kitty was right," Mary murmured. "It was all about money."

"Looks that way. But I'm not going to play their game." He turned her so that he could hold her in his arms, and rested his chin on top of her head. "I should somehow be able to get custody of Cruise without caving to this scheme Mother has apparently cooked up with Steffie's boyfriend."

"I thought he was going to marry her."

Jake snorted. "Looks like that was only to impress the judge. El Creepo says he's not going to marry Steffie unless he gets the money he loaned Mother." He rolled his eyes. "Mother has damned expensive taste and he paid off a couple of creditors for her, it seems."

"Oh, no," she murmured.

"Oh, yes. Sounds like she's run through everything my father left her." He shrugged. "I don't mean to sound callous, but if I pay this guy off, he's not going to marry Steffie, she's still going to have custody when he ditches her, and Cruise is still going to be traumatized. So I'd lose a lot of money and not get Cruise after all.''

"Unless you made that part of the agreement." Mary looked up at him. "Steffie only got temporary custody. Could you pay him something—I'm sure he doesn't expect a million dollars—" that was more money than Mary could really imagine "—on the assurance that you get full custody?"

He considered that before shaking his head. "No. I want this over and done with legally. My lawyer advises me that paying him off will just make matters worse. The jerk will always hang around for more, and I'll be paying for the rest of my life. I can't see how that could be good for Cruise. He may be a kid, but I'm positive he knows that man is no real father to him."

"I'm sure he does," Mary murmured. She stroked Jake's biceps, trying to soothe him. "Let's put our heads together on this. Two heads are better than one."

"I can't think right now."

He was upset, kicked into emotional overdrive by Steffie's call. Mary pulled him toward the kitchen. "I saw that Swinnie left some pie for you. Let's eat, and then I'm sure something will come to us."

"I hope so. I feel ill. I thought I was going to jump through the phone and throttle my sister."

Mary cut him a nice thick piece of pie. "This pie is so loaded with sugar that your very corpuscles will turn bright red from glucose shock. You'll perk up instantly whether you want to or not."

"Thanks, Doctor." Though his tone was slightly sarcastic, he was beginning to wear a smile.

"You're welcome," she said saucily, her mind going a mile a minute.

"Steffie said Cruise spilled all her perfume and virtually destroyed her makeup in less than five minutes. While his father was watching TV, his golf ball collection was taking a sail in the bathtub. He figured that out when water started leaking through the floor."

Mary looked up, catching the amusement in Jake's eyes before the worry clouded it. "I hope Cruise isn't going to suffer a lot of wrath."

"I thought about that, too, but El Creepo doesn't dare lay a hand on him. Cruise would be screaming and banged up at the next hearing and that would not impress the judge." Mary thought the only way to describe the satisfaction on Jake's face would be to use the word *smirk*. "Cruise has an enormous capacity for destruction. I think that's what accelerated the call from Steffie."

A grin broke out on Jake's face. Understanding dawned on Mary.

"You knew he'd be back up to his old tricks. You knew he'd destroy everything in sight."

"After I thought through any possible consequences, I *hoped*," he admitted. "I think her boyfriend being mad all the time will make Steffie quickly figure out that he didn't come back for love."

"He won't take it out on her?" Mary couldn't help worrying.

"Not as long as he thinks he's got me where he wants me." The smile slid from Jake's face to be replaced by anger. "This was never about Cruise, and I knew that. That's what makes me so mad."

She reached to guide his hand to his fork. "I'm comforted by the fact that you had a plan all along. Here I thought we were adrift."

He shook his head, taking a huge forkful of pie. "That was something I learned from Kitty. She told me once that being without proper preparation was foolhardy." His head jerked up as he realized what he'd said. "I forgot about preparation!"

Mary furrowed her brow. "What do you mean?"

"Condoms. Birth control. Cruise-prevention. I'm as irresponsible as my sister," he said with a groan.

She went on blithely eating pie.

"Did you hear me?" he demanded. "I might have gotten you pregnant!"

"I'm never without a plan." She sent him a shrewd look. "You should have learned that about me by now. You learned something from Kitty, but not a basic tenet of *my* personality. I don't think I like that."

He looked so confused that she felt sorry for him.

"Did you have a plan?" he asked cautiously.

"I went on the pill not long after I met you."

His jaw sagged. "You did?"

She nodded, supremely pleased by his astonishment. "While you were busy being noble about not sleeping with me, I was busy planning on making sure you were forced to overcome your lofty ethics."

"I see," he said, his voice somewhat stunned. "You succeeded admirably."

"I always do when I have a plan. You had a plan in case you didn't get custody. I say it's time we do some planning together." Mary put down her fork, feeling sugar-fortified enough to face mutual planning.

He nodded, meeting her gaze. "I think you're right. Brainstorm away."

"I was hoping you'd say that. I'm just out of ideas right now." That was the problem. She'd run out of inspiration.

V-room, v-rooom! interrupted her lack of inspiration. Mary raised her brows. "That sounds like a motorcycle."

Jake got up and Mary followed him. He halted, apparently not sure who should open the door. She shrugged and did it, her mouth opening in amazement. "It's the easy-rider med student," she said, awed by the tall figure standing on the porch. "Hi, Richard."

"Hi," he replied from under the helmet. He took it off, revealing an astonishingly handsome face and earnest eyes. "I've lost Rachel. Can you tell me where I can find her?"

"You've *lost* Rachel?" Jake echoed sternly. "She's been in Sunflower for weeks, and you show up to say you lost her? I oughta—"

Mary elbowed him to shut up. "My sister's not here."

"Oh." He looked terribly down about that. "I was hoping to see her. I need to…to apologize for something."

She eyed the man. He had dark hair which rested against his nape, slightly curled into place by the pressure of the helmet he'd worn. There was restlessness in his eyes, but caring, too. There was also a lot of sex appeal under that wide black jacket. Having made love with Jake, Mary could easily see what had compelled Rachel to jump on the back of Richard's bike.

"Tell me something," she said slowly. "Did you marry my sister? Last I heard, the two of you were riding off into elopement sunset."

"We are getting married," he replied with determination and a steely glint in his eye. "After Rachel understands about our misunderstanding."

"Oh." Mary was impressed with his focus but thought she saw a small area which needed adjustment. "Can I give you one small word of advice? As a future sister-in-law and fellow doctor?"

He nodded. "Sure."

"You and Rachel get married, after *you* understand about *your* misunderstanding."

"Oh." He thought about that for a moment before grinning. "Gotcha."

"Great. Now here's an address where you can find her. I'm not guaranteeing any results, mind you."

"I am. I take medicine as well as I dispense it."

She was satisfied. She handed him the piece of paper. "Keep the Hippocratic Oath."

"We'll send you an announcement." He happily jammed his helmet back on and ran to his motorcycle.

Jake put his arm around her as they watched him roar off. "I wasn't going to let him go that easily."

"I didn't," she murmured. "You have to understand about the Hippocratic Oath."

"You'll have to teach me."

"Okay. One of the tenets is that 'my colleagues will be as my family.'"

"I'd be willing to bet you had Rachel's heart more

on your mind than Easy Rider being part of your medical family.''

She smiled, not really thinking about teaching Jake anything anyway. She had a lot to learn from *him*. Thoughts were boiling in her mind. Rachel was going to be so happy to see her bikeman. Whatever had caused them pain was about to be put right. And it hadn't really taken a plan, a quantifiable goal. Her sister had been willing to take the chance, to jump onto a vehicle with no doors, and hang on for a ride into a Technicolor sunset to be with the man she loved. Yes, they'd hit a bump in the road, but in the end, it was all still going to work out.

Maybe Mary needed more gut instinct and less of a plan.

"Jake," she said in slow wonder, "you're never going to believe this, but I've got a super-duper, mega-mammoth idea.''

"I actually don't find that a huge leap."

She gazed up at him. "I should marry you, Jake. Now.''

Chapter Sixteen

Jake didn't see where that fit into a logical and ordered plan. "That *is* a leap. Why should you marry me now?"

She thought about Rachel. "Because it's impulsive." She thought about Esther and her epic plans. "And it's exciting." Mostly, she thought about Jake and Cruise and how she'd known deep in her heart that the judge wasn't going to award custody to a bachelor uncle instead of biological parents. But maybe a wife could tip the scales of justice in Jake's favor.

And that's when she knew she was definitively, overwhelmingly, irretrievably in love with Jake Maddox. *Name the town after him, Kitty, I'm gonna do exactly what you wanted.*

"I'm sorry. Could you get Mary for me, please? She was here a moment ago, and now some loony woman's impersonating her."

"Stop," Mary said, laughing. "What's so crazy about being impulsive and outrageous?"

"Because it's not you. You're faking it."

"No, I'm not. I'm changing my plan. Adjusting it."

"I like you just the way you are. I always have. Even before Swinnie and Kitty advertised your great legs in that red get-up." He ran one hand through her long hair. "I don't want you to change right now. I need one thing that's constant in my life."

"Are you saying you don't want to marry me?"

The laughter died from her eyes. She actually looked kind of perplexed, which Jake thought was cute. "I'm not saying that at all."

"You just want to rent my house and have great sex with me when I'm in from California?"

"I'm saying you're deviating from your plan, and it's not going to work," he said softly. "Stay on the track, Mary."

"But I don't think I want to anymore."

He drew her into his arms. "What did you say was in Swinnie's pie? Could the sugar have fermented to 120 proof?"

"You're not taking me seriously. I want you to."

Sighing, he kissed her nose. "Tomorrow, you are getting on that plane and you are not coming back. Even if Kitty calls you and tells you some dramatic story to lure you back, please do not return to Sunflower. Do you understand?"

"Understand that you never want to see me again?" she asked piteously.

He shook his head. "I am telling you that I will not marry you under these circumstances. You are not like your sisters, who tend to be more capricious. I would buy you any kind of motorcycle you want, but you'd regret riding away from your dream. You are who you are, and I have told you I am willing to wait for you. I can be very patient. Outside the bed."

"Jake, we said we were going to work together," she pleaded. "I want to help you."

"I know. That's one of the things that makes you so beautiful, Mary. You want to help everyone. You're a natural-born healer." He ran his palms over her shoulders and lifted her hair so that he could kiss her neck. "I'm patient, not a patient, sweetheart," he murmured against her skin.

Shivers ran down Mary's back. "Eat two pieces of pie. That might make you sick."

He laughed. "Maybe, but I still wouldn't let you stay. You have to go."

"I can't. Everything I want is here."

"No. It's not." Shaking his head, he said, "Follow the plan."

"What about Cruise?"

"I don't know about that." Jake shrugged, but Mary knew how much he was hurting inside. "It's out of my hands. Even if I was married, the judge isn't going to change his mind right now. I have to ride this out, and you might as well be doing what you need to do."

"We should be together," she insisted.

"I'm sorry. I've decided I can't marry anything less than a full-fledged doctor. It won't do me any good if your medical degrees are hanging in my laundry room."

"Jake!" She nipped his shoulder.

"Well, what children are you going to cure here in Sunflower?" he demanded.

"I thought we were going to be a team to help you get Cruise back. That's one child I can doctor."

"I love you for caring, but I have to do this on my own." He set her away from him. "But come get back in bed with me. I want to thank you properly for being such a wonderful woman."

"I think I'm getting the consolation prize."

He tugged her down the hall. "I promise you that by the time you see the dawn tomorrow, you'll feel fully consoled."

IT TOOK ALL of Jake's mental concentration and will of heart to put Mary on the plane the next day. He'd loved her all night long, hoping he'd be worn out to the point he could say goodbye to her without his world rocking under his feet.

His efforts failed him. The lovemaking was earth-shattering, he felt large countries inside his body move, but when she burst into tears boarding the plane, his whole world imploded.

Yet, he knew he'd done the right thing. She had worked too hard for too long to throw it all away now. When she'd asked him to marry her, it was all he could do not to jump into the air with a victory yell. Calmly, he'd told himself she would always regret what she'd given up. And he'd turned her down.

What he hadn't told her, though, was that he was leaving Sunflower. His bags were already packed; he'd give his notice to Kitty so he wouldn't have to tell Mary. While Mary slept, he quietly put his and Cruise's clothes in the trunk. The rest he'd come back for another time.

He was moving to Austin to be closer to Cruise.

Whenever he could get time with his nephew, he would. He hoped the judge might award him partial custody if he had a residence in the same city. Right now, that hope kept him from falling apart.

But he couldn't ask Mary to give up her dreams to straighten out his. And he sure couldn't ask her to move to Austin because of Cruise. She would have done it in a heartbeat.

He watched until the plane taxied down the runway. Then he got in his car and headed toward Austin. When she was safely returned to where she belonged, he would tell her the truth.

It had to be over between them.

JAKE CALLED KITTY when he got to the motel in Austin. He'd find an apartment or a duplex tomorrow, some place where he could swim and play with Cruise if he ever got to see him. Right now, though, he had to let down a very special group of people.

"Kitty," he said when she answered, "it's Jake."

"How are you doing?" she demanded. "We've all been wondering. Mary left us a message that she was going back."

"She flew to California today."

There was a slight pause. "I figured she wouldn't be able to get away from the ER too long."

"No. She couldn't." Jake drew in a deep breath. "Kitty, listen. I can't thank you enough for coming to Austin. Even though I knew how it was all going to turn out, there for a minute, with all of you behind me, I almost began to think I stood a shot."

"We wouldn't have missed it." Her tone was no-nonsense. "You're one of us."

He scrubbed at his scalp, not wanting to say what he had to say. "Being one of you felt fine, Kitty. I've never been happier. But...I've moved out of Sunflower Acres."

She didn't say anything. Jake squeezed the pencil he picked up off the cheap nightstand until he realized he was about to break it. "I'm going to live in Austin so I'll have a better chance of seeing Cruise. I intend to continue paying rent for the year lease we agreed on, unless you decide to rent the house out to someone else. I don't want to leave Mary with an empty place, but I have to be here now."

"I don't think that'll be a problem." She hesitated a moment. "Mary doesn't know, does she?"

"No." There wasn't much else he could say about that. It wasn't the way Mary would have wanted it. She would rather have moved to Austin and lived his dream. Lived his needs instead of sticking to her plan. He'd always know she'd given it up because of him.

"She could do residency in Austin."

"Maybe. They're tough to get, though, and she's near the end of the program."

A long silence indicated Kitty was thinking his words through. "That's true enough," she admitted reluctantly.

"I'll call her and tell her...maybe tomorrow."

He heard a deep sigh from the other end of the line. "Keep in touch with us, Jake. We want everything to work out for you."

"I will." He forced his voice to remain steady.

"Call us."

"I will."

"Give 'em hell."

"I'll try." His throat tightened. "Goodbye, Kitty. Tell everyone I said thanks."

"Will do."

The line cut off, and Jake hung up slowly. He looked out the hotel window, staring into the darkness.

More than anything, he wished Mary was with him.

"EMERGENCY MEETING," she announced to Swinnie. "Get over here fast. You get Tom. I'll get Bert."

In fifteen minutes, the foursome sat staring into the darkness outside Kitty's screened-in back porch.

"We gave it our best effort," Tom muttered.

"Mary won't ever come back now," Swinnie said sadly. "Eve is gone. Rachel's gone. Joan is gone. The twins are gone. And in a few months, Esther the baby will be gone. We failed at our mission."

"Guess there's no resurrecting Sunflower." Bert sagged in his chair. "What's the point of being mayor if there's only thirteen people to mayor?" He leaned back and stared at his feet. "Aw, heck, I didn't do anything anyway. Except fish."

"You did lots." Kitty patted his hand. "You're a fine representative for our town." What was left of it. "He said he'd call Mary tomorrow."

"Oh, dear." Swinnie shook her head. "Poor Mary. At least he didn't tell her before she left."

"I think that was the point. He wanted her to leave and go on with her life. She has her concerns, and he's got plenty on his plate, and the two simply don't mix." Kitty sighed. "What breaks my heart is that Mary didn't fly all the way back here to do a favor for Jake. She did it because she's in love with him.

And Jake knew she'd make every sacrifice to be with him and Cruise. He never felt he could allow her to do that for him." She sighed heavily. "If Jake had only been able to keep custody, Mary and Jake could have stuck to their plans. They'd be married by spring, darn that dadgum judge."

"Is it tampering with the court or something illegal like that if we go talk to the judge?" Bert wanted to know.

Kitty was impatient with Bert's turtle-slow thought process. If there was a solution, she wanted to hear it fast. "And just what would you say to him?"

"I don't know. That we got good fishing here in Sunflower, dang it!" Bert shouted, put out at having his idea run down. "It's a fine place to raise a family the old-fashioned way!"

For a moment, a battle light appeared in Kitty's eyes. Then she shook her head. "I think we'd best put a halt to meddling. There's only so much four old people can do." Her three friends stared at her in astonishment, but Kitty didn't care. It was true. She'd done her best. Now she was running up the white flag of surrender.

TEN MINUTES LATER, Jake got a phone call he wasn't expecting. "How did you get this number, Kitty?"

"Tom put this whirligig on my phone that shows who's calling," Kitty said succinctly. "I didn't want an answering machine, so he tinkered with this thing and what do you know, he actually got it to work. Last week he messed around with one of those chips that go into the TV somehow and now I've got free cable. I'm pretty sure that's illegal, but Tom likes getting gadgets to work. Just when you think all he does it sit around clicking his teeth, he gets some new project going. Anyway, this thingamabob recorded your number.''

It was ten o'clock and Jake was ready to hit the hay before he declared war on his mother tomorrow. ''What's on your mind?''

''Remember that gumshoe extraordinaire I mentioned? The one you wouldn't let me put on the case?''

He had hoped it wouldn't be necessary to play rough with his family, so he had politely turned Kitty's offer down. ''I remember. I probably should have let you hire him.''

She coughed delicately. ''I did.''

He raised his brows.

''Mind you, it was just a little something. I just wanted him to check out Cruise's father in a small way. You know, it didn't seem quite right to hand him over to a perfect stranger. And I'd checked you out, hadn't I? Didn't seem right not to—''

''All right, Miss Kitty. I'm not mad. What did he turn up?''

''You're not going to like this,'' she warned.

''I'm not exactly flat on my back from surprise about that.''

''Okay.'' There was a long pause on the other end of the line. ''Cruise's father is playing your family from both ends of the street.''

Jake rubbed his brow. ''Meaning?''

''That he's dating your sister and your mother.''

He sat up in the bed, totally listening now. ''I find that difficult to believe.''

Kitty sighed. "I would assume so. He's been very cagey about it. He dropped Steffie and Cruise off last night on the porch. After they went inside, he parked his car down the street and headed to the back door, where a woman fitting your mother's description let him in. Of course, maybe he's not really *dating* her in the literal sense, but he did stay overnight. In the morning, he returned to his condo. Later, he went to pick Cruise and Steffie up again."

Jake thought he might be sick.

"I hope you won't think badly of me," Kitty said softly. "I only meant for him to check on Cruise's well-being, actually. I was so afraid that…well, it's unthinkable. But my old suspicious mind just works and works, and I—"

"Kitty, I'm angry as hell, but not at you. I don't know why I didn't hire a detective myself." He was going to have a no-holds barred discussion with his mother first thing. And if Rat-face happened to be around and said one word to him, Jake just hoped he could retain enough of his sanity not to kill him. "I'd better talk to your detective friend and make sure I've got all the details."

"He thought you might want to give him a call."

She rattled off a number which he scribbled on hotel stationery. "Thank you."

"You're welcome. I sure do hope you'll bring Cruise back to Sunflower, Jake. Y'all are part of us, you know."

She hung up. Jake sat frozen, the receiver in his hand.

IF HE WERE CIVILIZED, he would wait until the morning—but Jake was over being civilized. Twenty minutes later, he slammed the car door and sprinted up the porch of his mother's house.

The butler answered. If he was surprised to see an unsmiling Jake standing there after ten years, he didn't let it show. "Good to see you, Jake."

"Thanks, George." His gaze sliced to the curving staircase. The detective had reported that his mother usually had company at this hour. It was prime time for a visit. "I assume Jean is upstairs?" He refused to call her mother ever again.

The butler's expression didn't change. "Yes, sir."

"Would she be entertaining company?"

"I believe so, sir. I am not to disturb her for any reason after ten."

"Excellent." Jake nodded, striding to the staircase. "You may hear loud noises, George. Ignore them."

"Absolutely."

Jake paused, one foot on the staircase. "Where is Cruise?"

"In the west wing with Steffie."

"See that neither he nor Steffie deviate from their usual routine and disturb Jean for any reason."

"I won't budge from here."

Jake nodded and turned.

"Nothing's been the same here since you left, Jake."

The grim expression on Jake's face lightened for a moment. "Cruise and I are moving, George. If you get a hankering for clean, country air, give me a call."

"I may do that."

"Good." Jake bounded up the stairs, banging on the closed bedroom door.

"George! I am not to be disturbed for any reason!" Jean's tone was peeved.

Jake threw the door open. His mother sat up in shock, clutching the sheets to her chest. Her lover leaped from the bed. He didn't bother to grab anything for modesty, probably thinking to give George a sound cursing for entering uninvited. Jake sent a cursory glance over her boyfriend, particularly the area between his legs. "Pathetic," he said.

"What are you doing here?" Jean demanded.

Rat-face realized he was under siege and jumped for his clothes.

"Coming to get what's mine." Jake folded his arms across his chest. "I want Cruise. I want him now."

"You can't have him." Steffie's boyfriend smirked. "The court says I have him until permanent custody arrangements are made."

"Look." Jake carelessly leaned against the door, his shoulders loose, his arms still crossed. "You may have a hearing problem. I may have to correct it for you. I am taking Cruise with me when I go. You are not his father. You are a slime that slithered into this house and found a willing slime partner in her—" Jake indicated Jean with his eyes "—but you are not going to hold an innocent little boy hostage while I have breath left in my body."

"Give me my million and you can have him."

"You know, I *am* going to have to kill you," Jake said, pushing himself away from the wall. "I was really hoping I wouldn't have to, especially not tonight."

"All right!" Rat-face held up two hands. "No need

to be unreasonable. Half a mil, and you never see me again."

"That won't be enough to pay off my debts," Jean complained, looking over at her boyfriend as he rapidly stuffed his shiny shirt into his pants.

"You'll have to find some other way to pay your debts." Rat-face barely glanced at her. "You spent the money, you pay for it."

She gasped. "You said you'd make sure I got everything—"

"—you had coming to you. And you have. Nothing." He turned to Jake. "Do we have a deal?"

Jake swallowed, warning his muscles not to react yet. "Write a letter telling the judge that you don't want custody."

"With what?"

Jake tossed him pen and paper off his mother's writing desk. "Make it good," he demanded. "Make it damn sincere."

Rat-face appeared to work very hard, as if it were his epitaph. Jake wished it *was* an epitaph. He flexed his fingers as he glanced over at his mother while her ex-boyfriend scribbled. "What's the matter with you, anyway?" he asked her. "What mutated your maternal gene?"

"I don't know what you mean!" she cried, sounding as if she was about to work herself into a soap-operatic fit.

"I know you don't. That's what's so pathetic." He snatched the paper from the slime and gave it a cursory glance. "Now get out. Actually, stay if you like. I really don't care." He turned and walked out the bedroom door, intensely sick of the entire matter.

"Hey, where's my money?" the boyfriend demanded, appearing behind Jake on the staircase.

Jake tucked the paper into his pocket for safekeeping. "You have a choice. Both choices involve the same ending, which is that I never see your face again. You either go back in there and hide until I leave, or I toss you out the window. How fast are you at making decisions?" He turned and put one foot on the staircase toward Cruise's sperm donor.

The man backed quickly into the bedroom and shut the door.

"Oh, good," Jake said to George who waited at the foot of the stairs. "He made a good choice, don't you think?"

"I do." George nodded enthusiastically.

"If Lame-brain up there calls the cops and says I forced him to do something against his will, be sure to put the bug in their ears about his history of bribery and petty felony, as well as his four different aliases to cover his trail of hot checks, if you don't mind." Kitty's pride in her gumshoe hadn't been misplaced.

"I will. And you should call on me as a witness to Cruise's treatment in the household if you should end up in court again, though I don't think it will be necessary."

Jake nodded, not liking what he was hearing. "I should have thought of calling on you before." He patted the elderly butler on the arm. "She's going to be impossible to work for now, and probably unable to pay you."

"I think I'll like fresh country air."

"Good. Sunflower Junction is a great place to live." Jake went down the hall. Sudden screeching from behind one of the doors made him throw it open with force.

Cruise was running around the room, jumping on and off the bed to elude Steffie. She was in hot pursuit, screeching at the top of her lungs. Cruise clutched a bra, black with gold accents, which he apparently intended to throw out the window except that he skidded to a stop when he saw Jake.

"Uncle Jake!" He dropped the bra and ran straight into his uncle's arms.

"What are you doing here?" Steffie demanded, snatching the tasteless undergarment off the floor.

"I've come to get Cruise. For good." His eyes glinted.

"Fine! I wish you would take the little monster!" she shrieked. "He nearly ruined a fifty-dollar brassiere!"

Jake shook his head. "Steffie, I wish you didn't have so much of your mother in you. It's sad." He glanced around the room, seeing that Cruise's suitcase had barely been unpacked, although the clothes were all mixed up inside as if Steffie had considered dressing him and given up. The shirt he wore didn't match his shorts, and he had on mismatched tennis shoes. His hair hadn't been combed.

"Come on, Cruise," he said, grabbing the suitcase as the little boy clung to his neck as if he were afraid Jake might disappear again, "let's color ourselves out of this comic strip."

"'Kay," Cruise agreed instantly. "I'll be Snoopy."

"Then I'll be Charlie Brown. Let's go see if Doctor Mary is in."

Cruise giggled against his neck as they got in the car. "Lucy."

"Mary's much nicer, don't you think?" He buckled Cruise in securely.

"Yeah. I like making birdfeeders."

"We'll have to fly on a plane to see Mary," Jake told him, hesitating suddenly as he remembered Cruise's abject fear of planes.

"Can I get wings? And peanuts?"

Jake smiled, reassured. "Snoopy usually gets what he wants, doesn't he?"

"Yeah!" Cruise laughed, reminded that he was Snoopy. "Charlie Brown doesn't."

Jake slid behind the wheel, hoping with all his heart Mary hadn't changed her mind after he'd sent her away. It was time to find out if the doctor was in—for him.

Chapter Seventeen

Jake called Kitty from his car phone despite the hour. "Did I wake you?"

"Do you honestly think I could sleep knowing that Austin was about to become Armageddon?" she demanded. "I knew in my bones you weren't going to wait until morning to get Cruise. Can I talk to him?"

He was astonished. "How do you know I have him?"

"Because you're a man of action," Kitty said simply. "Let me hear his sweet little voice."

Jake grinned as he passed the phone to Cruise. They talked for a couple of minutes, then he got the phone back.

"Sure is good to hear the little fellow's voice," Kitty said with a happy sigh.

"It's even better to hold him. I think he's grown in the couple of days we've been apart." Jake tucked the phone under his ear and reached over to pat Cruise's hand, though the child didn't seem to need any reassurance. He seemed happy just to be with Jake.

"Are you bringing him home to Sunflower?" Kitty demanded.

He laughed. "Yes. But I'm making a detour by way of California first. Cruise wants to see the ocean, don't you, buddy?"

Cruise nodded happily.

Kitty was joyous. "Bring my family back to me, Jake."

"I will, Miss Kitty, if she says yes."

"Says...yes?" Kitty sounded as if fireworks had just gone up in her sky. "To a marriage proposal?"

"I hope so." He thought of his family's self-centered lives, and how he hadn't let Mary get close to him because he didn't feel he deserved her. "I'm not an educated man, Miss Kitty, and that's always bothered me. But I learned two things tonight. First, I'm a fool not to grab that special lady and never let her go. Second, I've been afraid to expect too much. But if she'll still have me, I'm going to make her Dr. Maddox."

"Doctor Maddox!" Kitty squealed. "I like the sound of that!"

"You know, I do, too," he said slowly, meaning it more every second as he ran it through his mind. "Dr. and Mr. Maddox. What do you think about that?"

"I think," Kitty said, her voice quivering with undisguised delight, "I think I've never been so happy in my whole life!"

MARY COULDN'T believe her eyes when she opened the door late that night to find Jake holding a sleeping Cruise in his arms.

"Oh, my stars!" she cried, throwing her arms around Jake's neck with delight, though she was careful not to wake Cruise. "What are you doing here?" she asked as she moved back.

Jake just stared at her as he stood in the hallway. Mary's heart did crazy somersaults inside her. Her hair was in a towel because she'd just finished showering, she'd thrown on a somewhat ratty velour robe she liked to study in, and yet, the glow in his eyes told her he liked what he saw anyway. She was so glad to see him—and yet, why didn't he seem happier for a man who'd flown across a few states to get to her door?

"Are you on the run with Cruise?" she demanded suddenly.

A real smile touched his lips. "Would it matter if I was?"

"Depends." She gestured for him to come inside. "I don't know if I have a big enough closet to hide you both in if the police come after you."

She watched as he gently laid Cruise on an overstuffed sofa. "Here," she said, handing him a blanket to put over the child. Jake pulled Cruise's shoes off, but the child didn't move a muscle.

"Out like a light," Jake said with satisfaction.

"Why do you have him?" she demanded. "Tell me everything."

He shook his head. "I will later. I am not on the run, though. Suffice to say, I reached the breaking point with the whole thing. The guy wanted my money, and I wasn't going to allow Cruise to be a pawn. I dropped a letter that Cruise's father wrote relinquishing his claim to custody at my lawyer's office on my way out of town. And I can assure you, Steffie won't do a thing to get him back. The whole bogus deal was orchestrated by her boyfriend, who had been very busy but not necessarily smart.'' He sighed heavily. "I did what had to be done.''

"You're my hero,'' she said softly. Tired lines radiated from Jake's eyes. The doctor in her noted his worn-out condition, but the woman in her wanted to hear everything. Wanted to touch Jake. Wanted to feel him close to her. She put her hand on his arm. "Why don't you sit down, let me get you a drink, and then…will you tell me why you're here?''

He didn't draw her to him as she'd hoped he would. He merely remained standing, as if what he had to say required his complete focus.

"I'm here to tell you I was wrong.''

"About what?'' she asked softly.

"You and me. Us.'' His gaze roamed her face anxiously. "I wasn't telling the truth when I told you not to come back to Sunflower. That wasn't the way I really felt.''

That surprised her. "It wasn't?''

"No. I didn't want you to leave. I could think of a million reasons why you should stay with me. But I told myself not to be a coward and to let you go.''

She read the indecision in his eyes, and it reassured her to know that he'd wanted her beside him after all. "And now?''

"And now I know I was a coward not to tell you how I really feel.'' He took a deep breath. "You offered me everything, Mary. I've been doing a lot of thinking about that, and I've put some things behind me. I'd like a second chance to accept what you were offering.''

"You would?" She raised her brows at him.

"Yes, I would. I don't feel right about you giving up your residency. But I don't feel right about not being with you, either. Cruise and I, we need you. I need you. Remember when you explained to Easy Rider where he was missing the road?''

She nodded, her eyes curious.

"I've been thinking a lot about what you said to him. It applies to me, too." He ran a hand through his hair, splaying the black ends as he sought the right words. "I know I told you I had to do everything on my own, but I shouldn't have left you out. Not when you mean more to me than anything."

Her heart nearly stopped in her chest. "What exactly are you saying?"

"I'm saying that I love you, Mary. And I want to be with you, whether it's in California or Sunflower Junction."

"Oh, my." All her breath left her suddenly. The change was so profound she reveled in it. "And the next time you decide you have to ride off into the sunset to solve something?''

"You go with me, if you want to."

She paused before saying, "And the next time I tell you I have a decision to make that involves my career?"

"You make it." He chopped the air horizontally with his hand to emphasize his point.

"Even when you think I should do things differently?" Her eyes narrowed on him slightly.

"I listen," he stated. "I will pay much better attention."

She pinched him lightly on the arm. "You're fibbing through your teeth."

"I may be exaggerating my compliance in every matter," he admitted. "I just want the best for you."

"And what if that's you? What if you are all I want?" she demanded.

He slowly drew her to him. "Then that's all you get." He lowered his lips to hers, hesitating. "And I will support your decision. Though it will bother me, you know, because a medical degree is—"

"All I ever wanted. And I want you, too, and Cruise. What do you have to say to that?"

"Be greedy," he whispered against her lips. "I'm in love with you, Mary van Doorn. I was crazy to think I could live without you."

"Good," she murmured, "because I've already turned in my notice on my residency."

"What?" he demanded, pulling back to stare down into her eyes. "What are you talking about?"

"I had no intention of staying out here. You thought you put me on that plane for good, but you don't know me very well if you think I was going to let you go that easily." She pointed her finger against his chest. "It took me a while to realize deviating from my plan might be a good thing, but once I got the hang of it, I decided I liked changing my focus."

He looked so upset Mary almost felt sorry for him.

"You're not going to finish your residency? I just think that's not—"

She shot him a warning look.

"I mean, I support your decision..."

"And?" she prompted.

"But it's giving up the chance of a lifetime. The dream of years of hard work, Mary," he protested. "I never even made it past—"

"We're not talking about you." She pinned him with her most serious expression. "It wasn't your dream. It was mine. And you say you are behind me. So let's hear your support."

He blew out a heavy breath and wrapped her more tightly in his arms. "I love you, Mary. I don't deserve you, but I'll spend every day of my life making you the most happy woman on earth."

She snuggled up to him for a kiss. "I love you, too. I have a doctor friend I used to work for who moved to Dallas. She offered me the opportunity to finish my residency there. So I jumped on the chance. I have to be with you, Jake."

He moved his head to stare down at her in surprise. "When were you going to tell me?"

"When you were finished with your Lone Ranger routine." She stopped his protest with a shake of her head. "You had to fix some things in your life. I understood. So I didn't tell you I was only coming back here to pack." She stared up at him longingly. "We belong together, no matter where it is. It's time to say yes to my proposal, Jake, because I've got plans for you."

"I like the sound of that." He kissed her, making her tingle from head to toe with the sudden emotion and need sweeping through her. "Tell me the plans."

"First you have to say yes," she instructed.

"Wait. I am a traditional guy in some senses,

though I support your decision to pop the question. But can I go first?''

She smiled. "Nothing would make me happier."

He gave her a light swat on the behind. "Mary, will you do me the great honor of becoming my wife, so that I can have you and hold you every night, and put up a sign at Sunflower Acres that says *Home of Dr. and Mr. Maddox?*"

Stars of happiness burst inside her. "Yes," she murmured. "Will you do me the honor of becoming my husband, so that I can have you and hold you every night, and marry me on the way back home in one of those drive-through chapels in Vegas?"

"I know I'm supposed to say yes," he stalled, "but may I hold out one last time for you to choose something more traditional? I support your suggestion," he amended quickly, "but I always said I would wait for you, Mary. I can wait long enough for a wedding blessed by a minister."

She laughed. "We can have a wedding with a minister when we get back to Sunflower. But I want to live a little impetuously and romantically. I want to relax the plan, color outside the lines some. With you."

"Do we need a motorcycle?"

"I've been here for two years so we're going to need to rent a truck to get to Texas. We can drive a truck through one of those instant wedding places, can't we?"

"We'll find out," he murmured against her cheek. "You know, it does sound kind of fun. But if you're worried about lack of romance with me, you're marrying the wrong guy. I intend to shower you with romance for the rest of our lives."

She sighed with happiness as she melted into his arms. "You know, I didn't plan on falling in love with you. But now that I have, I know why my parents were always so happy together." She smiled up at him, her eyes full of love. "I'm going to enjoy being Dr. Maddox."

His eyes shone. "I'm going to enjoy making you Dr. Maddox." He nodded toward Cruise. "And I'm going to enjoy adopting him. The three of us belong together."

"Do you think he'll be all right with this?" For the first time, Mary's eyes clouded. "Us getting married?"

"He told me on the way out here that he hoped you'd come back to Sunflower. He says you've got a lot more things to do with him. Cruise likes to stay busy."

"He's such a good boy," Mary said decisively. "We'll be a very happy family."

"Yes, we will." Jake lingered over her lips before he brushed them lightly. "Tomorrow we locate the drive-through chapel, complete with an Elvis-dressed minister if you want, and get started being the Maddox family."

Mary gave herself up to the wonder and magic of being in Jake's arms, and knowing this time that it was forever.

"It's a plan," she whispered, before they melded together in a sweetly thrilling kiss.

Epilogue

At Sunflower Acres, Mary and Jake's wedding day bloomed bright as anyone could want, which Kitty decided was a heavenly smile on the marriage. A light breeze ruffled the air, keeping the guests comfortable and the bride serene at the perfection of the afternoon.

Cruise hopped happily after grasshoppers in the field, only slightly rumpling his black-and-white ringbearer's tux. The rings were securely tied to the pillow he poked at an errant grasshopper or two. The child loved living at the farm. Mary and Jake were delighted with the change in his behavior. Cruise's future boded well, Kitty thought with satisfaction as she stood beside Swinnie.

The two of them were serving as matrons of honor, while Tom and Bert escorted Mary to the makeshift altar at the edge of the sunflower fields. She kissed each man's leathery cheek and thanked them, just as a good girl might thank her father for raising her properly before giving her away.

Kitty grinned as Mary and Jake exchanged a kiss before the minister began the service, in keeping with

Mary's occasional bent for straying outside the lines of protocol.

"Doesn't Mary look lovely?" Swinnie whispered.

"She most certainly does. Jake cuts quite a dashing figure himself," she whispered back. "And the girls are most beautiful. They do us proud."

The six sisters stood to the side of Mary, radiant in long ivory dresses, each holding a bouquet of small sunflowers, white daisies and baby's breath. Kitty cast a quick eye over Esther's face, noting that she'd managed to wash off every single trace of yellow paint. My, but that child had given the water tower a design the townspeople would be admiring for years. Where the other girls had left their graduation years emblazoned, Esther had painted large bright sunflowers. The sisters had obviously helped because they still wore the effects of the cobalt undercoat in tiny flecks on their hair and under their nails. Privately, Kitty felt that the girls had done a good thing by making up for defacing public property all those years. *Good seeds grow to become good plants.*

And if Swinnie, Tom and Bert thought she hadn't noticed the specks of blue paint in the men's ears and lightly frosting Swinnie's hair, they needed to have their heads examined. She never missed a trick. Why, they'd helped Esther put herself into danger, even if it was for a Michelangelo of a masterpiece! After she saw Mary and Jake off into the sunset of happy endings, she intended to wring the entire story out of her buddies and let them know they'd have to get up a lot earlier in the morning to fool her.

Esther, forever the baby van Doorn, my baby. Homecoming night Esther had been elected Queen, wearing the same crown each of her sisters had worn. Then she'd announced to the family that she was going to Italy to study art after she graduated. Kitty would have preferred another medical degree in the family, but as she squinted toward the water tower, she had to admit the yellow sunburst effect on top was pretty impressive. Quite a tourist attraction the youngest van Doorn had created for Sunflower Junction. All the girls were special, perhaps going different ways than she might have wished at first, but in the end making her justifiably satisfied.

Mary wore a traditional wedding gown with long, see-through lace sleeves, ankle-button boots, and a length of tulle which brushed her shoulders when the breeze teased at it.

"I know the van Doorns are looking down upon this moment with tears of happiness in their eyes," Kitty told Swinnie.

"Yes," Swinnie agreed. "You know, there was a time when I thought Mary was contrary. And her sisters irascible at moments."

"I know." Kitty smiled, her eyes filling with sentimental tears at the happy memories. Her gaze settled on her tall, wonderful Mary. "Mary, Mary, quite contrary, how does your garden grow?" she murmured.

"Mary's not contrary anymore," Swinnie noted with pride.

"No. And she grew her garden with love and understanding. Those sisters of hers will never know how lucky they are."

"But we do," Swinnie said, hugging her friend.

"Yes," Kitty sighed with satisfaction. "We most certainly do." She perked up at the sudden thought the wedding had brought to mind. "Remember that farmhouse I was going to show to Jake a while back?"

Swinnie bobbed her head. "Yes."

"I wrote a contract on it this morning. A big family with seven sons thinks it's just perfect."

"Seven sons?" Swinnie was duly impressed. "Marriage-age?"

"No," Kitty said with a conspiratorial smile. "Children. To kick-start Mary's practice in Sunflower."

"Ah," Swinnie breathed. "Patients for Mary."

"No," Kitty said decisively. "Playmates for Cruise! And population for Sunflower Junction," Kitty said with a happy sigh. "The sign numbers increase from now on!"

They glanced at each other with delighted smiles before watching the happy wedding couple exchange a kiss.

"Let's get Tom and Bert packed up for a night-time fishing trip after the wedding. It's time we teach Cruise how to fish," Kitty suggested.

"You don't care a thing about fishing."

"No, but I care about Mary and Jake spending some time alone together so they can enjoy a proper wedding night. Or two."

Swinnie smiled. "It was nice of Jake not to make us keep to our offer of naming the town after him. Think we should let him know we intend to keep our part of the bargain if he wants us to?"

"No." Kitty watched the sisters spatter Mary and Jake with sunflower seeds. "He never wanted anything from Sunflower except Mary. She was the cream of the crop, and he knew that from the moment he first laid eyes on her.'' She smiled up at the heavens happily, knowing her friends were watching. ''We're so fortunate that you shared your seeds of love and respect. Thank you, thank you, thank you, for planting your garden in Sunflower Junction!''

Mary came to kiss her goodbye, with Jake at her side. ''Thank you, Miss Kitty,'' she said, giving her a big hug and kiss. ''I'm so glad you chose this wonderful man for me.''

Kitty shook her head. ''He came to Sunflower on his own. He would have found you sooner or later.''

''With your help, it was sooner,'' Mary said with a laugh. Jake pressed her to his side, and Mary thought she would die of happiness.

''You're supposed to be getting in the car and driving off into the sunset. Tom and Bert are keeping an eye on Cruise. What's the hold-up?'' Kitty demanded, not wanting them to see the sentimental tears in her eyes.

''We just wanted to thank you. And kiss you all goodbye.''

Kitty waved her toward the car. ''Thank us by enjoying a few nights to yourselves.''

Jake helped Mary into the car. He slid in beside her. ''Where to?'' he asked.

''Anywhere I can be with you,'' she said. And it was true. The sun was shining, Jake was next to her, and Mary's heart was filled with joy. ''Look!'' she exclaimed, pointing to a silver shower of light sparkling in the pink-lit sky.

They gazed at each other as the astonishing twinkles slowly faded.

"What do you suppose that was?" she asked Jake.

"I'm not sure," he said, squeezing her hand. "Though I've seen it once before."

"Really? When?"

"When I was trying to decide where to live with Cruise. I was driving around looking for property, and when I saw *Welcome to Sunflower Junction,* all of a sudden there was a misting of light." He shrugged with a smile. "At the time, I thought I'd gotten caught in some kind of pop-up sun shower or something." He brushed a kiss across her lips that made her shiver with anticipation and happiness. "Now I know it was leading me to the treasure at the end of the rainbow."

"Jake, I love you so much," Mary told him.

"I love you," he replied. "I'm going to spend the rest of my life showing you how much."

The best kind of treasure is in the heart, she thought to herself as they gazed into each other's eyes. The prescription was to be willing to give it away, which in some miraculous way led to keeping that treasure—forever.

LOOK OUT FOR SOME FAST AND LOOSE MATCHMAKING FROM

Cathy Gillen Thacker once again brings
her special brand of down-home romance
to a *new* four-book miniseries

John and Lilah McCabe have four of the sexiest
sons Laramie, Texas, has ever seen—but no
grandbabies! Now they're fixin' to get a whole
passel of 'em.

September 1999—#789 **DR. COWBOY**
Cathy's 50th Harlequin book!

October 1999—#793 **WILDCAT COWBOY**

November 1999—#797 **A COWBOY'S WOMAN**

December 1999—#801 **A COWBOY KIND OF DADDY**

Round 'em up at a store near you!

 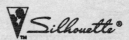

 **HARLEQUIN®**
Makes any time special ™

WIN A DREAM

In celebration of Harlequin®'s golden anniversary

Enter to win a *dream!* You could win:

- A luxurious trip for two to
  The Renaissance Cottonwoods Resort
  in Scottsdale, Arizona, or
- A bouquet of flowers once a week for a year
  from **FTD**, or
- A $500 shopping spree, or
- A fabulous bath & body gift basket, including
  K-tel's *Candlelight and Romance* 5-CD set.

Look for **WIN A DREAM** flash on
specially marked Harlequin® titles by
Penny Jordan, Dallas Schulze,
Anne Stuart and Kristine Rolofson
in October 1999*.

FTD

**RENAISSANCE.
COTTONWOODS RESORT**
SCOTTSDALE, ARIZONA

K·TEL

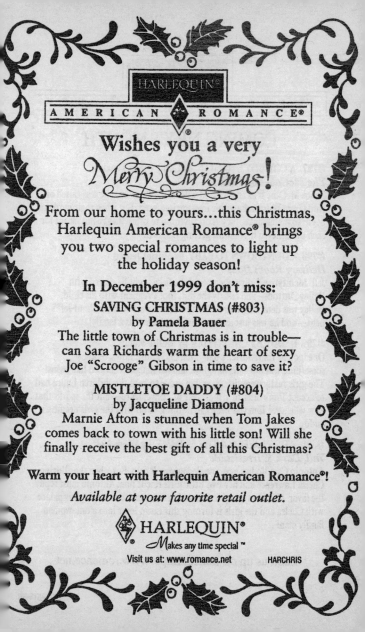

COMING NEXT MONTH

#797 A COWBOY'S WOMAN by Cathy Gillen Thacker
The McCabes of Texas
Shane McCabe is as rugged and wild as the Texas land he was raised on.
And Greta Wilson shares his free-spirited ways. But when their mothers
begin to matchmake, they'll do anything to prove they're not meant for
each other...even if it means getting married!

#798 COUNTDOWN TO BABY by Muriel Jensen
Delivery Room Dads
Jeff McIntyre vividly remembered the fiery night he shared with
Bailey Dutton—and clearly she did, too! Pregnant with his child,
Bailey was determined to make it to the delivery room without Jeff's
help—and he was just as determined to leave it as a family!

#799 DADDY BY CHRISTMAS by Mollie Molay
One look at Tom Aldrich's daughter, and Laura Edwards knew
something was up—*his* daughter and *her* daughter looked like twins!
The girls really were sisters, and in order to keep the children Laura had
to accept Tom's offer of a marriage of convenience—but the sparks that
flew whenever Tom was near had nothing to do with the girls needing a
daddy....

#800 THE PLAYBOY & THE MOMMY by Mindy Neff
Tall, Dark & Irresistible
Antonio Castillo has never needed anyone's help. But when the alluring
Chelsa Lawrence and her two little girls rescue him, Antonio must repay
the favor. He's always had a woman in every port, but sharing his palace
with Chelsa and the girls is turning this Latin lover into a one-woman
family man!

Look us up on-line at: http://www.romance.net